"Elizabe[...]

Lizzie had known his voice instantly. What she
didn't know was why he was calling her after three
years. She remembered clearly her last words to
him: *If you change your mind, call me.* Well, the
statute of limitations had run out on changes of
mind.

"What do you want?" she asked him, hoping he'd get
to the point quickly.

He chuckled. "I want you to help me build a
haunted house."

Oh, he did, did he? "I'm sorry, I can't. I just don't
have time to help you."

There was a short silence. "Is business so good you
can afford to turn down a fee because you're
bitter?"

"Actually, it is." And she was delighted to tell him
so. She started to say goodbye, but he interrupted
her.

"Think, Elizabeth. You'd be in charge. You could
boss me around and make my life miserable. Here's
your chance...are you woman enough to take it?"

Heather Allison lives in Houston, Texas, with her electrical-engineer husband and two live-wire sons. A former music teacher who traded a piano keyboard for a computer keyboard, she enjoys researching her books and is not above involving her family. They especially liked touring haunted houses for *HAUNTED SPOUSE* and even designed and operated one in their neighborhood. The boys suggest that future stories revolve around food, video games and extended school holidays. Heather threatens to write one about sons who do all the cooking and housework.

Books by Heather Allison

HARLEQUIN ROMANCE
3091—DECK THE HALLS
3157—PULSE POINTS
3218—JACK OF HEARTS
3269—IVY'S LEAGUE

HAUNTED SPOUSE
Heather Allison

Harlequin Books

TORONTO • NEW YORK • LONDON
AMSTERDAM • PARIS • SYDNEY • HAMBURG
STOCKHOLM • ATHENS • TOKYO • MILAN
MADRID • WARSAW • BUDAPEST • AUCKLAND

To my in-laws, Edward and Ruth Ann MacAllister,
who are not at all scary.

Boo! to the Providence Babysitting Co-op from your
former haunted-house chairman.

Special thanks to Leonard Pickel of Elm Street
Hauntrepreneurs in Irving, Texas, for his insights into
the haunted-house business. Any deviations from
accepted haunting practices are mine alone.

And to Pat Kay, Alaina Richardson, Elaine Kimberley
and Marilyn Amann for their frightfully good critiques.

ISBN 0-373-03284-6

Harlequin Romance first edition October 1993

HAUNTED SPOUSE

CHAPTER ONE

LIZZIE WILCOX SCREAMED.

A hideously deformed mummy glowed in a weak orange light, then slipped through a hidden door, slamming it behind him. Maniacal laughter taunted her as the orange light winked out, leaving her in total darkness.

She waited for her racing heart to slow before tentatively reaching to the side, her fingers crawling along a wall until it veered sharply and disappeared.

She waved back and forth. Nothing. Just an ominous blackness. She crept forward, groping in the dark. She could see nothing. Good.

She took one step. Then another.

Then jumped as a blast of icy air licked her legs.

Trying to catch her balance, Lizzie flailed her arms in the inky black before finding a hold on something warm. Something furry.

Something growling.

She shrieked, blindly twisting away. At that moment, a green glow illuminated another hallway. The growling next to her had turned into a roar, so she ran.

As soon as she entered the hallway, the moaning began.

She was in a dungeon, and these were the cells of lost souls. Transparent wraithlike figures wavered in the air, their skin leathered and wrinkled. She could smell the musty odor of ancient, rotting clothes and hear rattling chains. And, of course, incessant moaning.

Lizzie rushed to the end of the hallway. In the last cell a figure on the far side of its room held up a glowing orb and beckoned to her. Even though she knew better, Lizzie walked up to the bars. She leaned close and suddenly the spirit appeared right in front of her face. He moaned in her ear.

She jumped back, too close to the cells on the opposite side of the hallway. Bony hands reached out to stroke her curly hair.

"No!" she yelled and raced from the green light into more blackness.

Suddenly the floor tilted. Stumbling, she turned another corner and heard her footsteps echo hollowly. She no longer stood on solid cement.

The floor glowed yellow. Looking down between the wooden slats, she saw fire, heard screams and felt pounding as monsters beat on the ceiling of their prison.

Moving as quickly as she dared, she rounded yet another corner.

Something sticky grazed her face. Lizzie brushed at the tenuous strands. "Oh, ick. I hate cobwebs!"

"Then leave," ordered a deep voice at her elbow.

Yelping, Lizzie ran through mist, spurred on by shrieks and screams until she emerged into blinding sunlight.

She blinked, eyes watering. The muggy heat of a Houston fall warmed her face and hands, reminding her that she hadn't applied sunblock this morning. Redheads, especially redheads living in south Texas, should never forget to apply sunblock.

Lizzie exhaled, tucking a bunch of wiry hair behind her ear.

"Well?" demanded a monk with a skull for a face. "How was it? How'd we do?"

"Did we get you?" asked a werewolf, rubbing hairy hands together.

Lizzie remembered her scream. They'd heard it, she knew they had. And they'd have realized it wasn't rehearsed like the rest of her reactions. "Yes, you got me," she admitted. "I wasn't expecting the orange fright zone."

"Awright!" More monsters appeared laughing and whooping. They ripped off their masks to reveal sweaty, and human, faces. "If we scared Lizzie, we'll scare everybody!"

"Hold it!" Lizzie called to get their attention. "In this case, I don't mind you altering my design, but let me show you why I didn't station a fright zone there."

Lizzie walked to the entrance of the Panhellenic Haunted House, Shrieks by Greeks, sponsored by the sororities and fraternities of Houston Junior College. The exuberant students who followed her were trying to raise money for a shelter for the homeless by running a haunted house during October. A sign—Being Homeless is Scary—dangled crookedly from a tree.

Lizzie, actually Elizabeth Wilcox of Elizabeth Wilcox Architects, specialized in designing spook houses and fun houses. For several months of the year she tried hard to scare people—to make their palms sweat, their hearts pound and their adrenaline rush.

Flipping on the lights inside the entrance to her latest complete design, Lizzie walked a twisting, turning path to a point near the center of the haunted house. "This is where you added the orange mummy, right?"

There were murmurs of assent, and the orange mummy peered out from behind the door.

Lizzie gestured. "Normally this remains closed because it conceals the people operating the mist for the other side."

"I'm also the mist operator," the mummy announced.

Lizzie nodded as she studied the door and the wall opposite it. "Do you think you can do both?"

"Sure," he replied with youthful optimism.

"I went through by myself," Lizzie pointed out. "Usually several groups tour at once. Their screams are heard by those behind them. That adds to their anticipation, their unease. You must time your scares on one side so you won't miss operating the mist on the other." She hesitated, not wanting to discourage their creativity. "You can do it if you're quick."

"Is that the only problem you found?" asked the werewolf.

"You were too late with the light on the other side of the cavern. You don't want people to stop and wait as long as I did. Remember—scare forward. You were a bit heavy-handed with the cobwebs and the exit sign wasn't illuminated. You'd better check that."

They nodded and she grinned. "Great dungeon scene, though. And what was that smell?"

"Our laundry," answered the monk.

"Very creative." Chuckling, Lizzie kicked and pounded at the walls around the mummy's fright zone. "The mummy has to pop in and out fast. We don't want anyone running into the door. They can't see it in the dark. Safety is your most important consideration." She kicked the walls again. "When the mummy appears, people are going to jump back and bash into this wall—just the way I did. It'll have to be reinforced."

Groans accompanied her statement. Lizzie laughed. "You've got time. You aren't opening until this weekend."

"We've got midterms," the monk said. "That's why we wanted to finish early. Are you sure the wall isn't strong enough as it is?"

"Maybe. Maybe not." Lizzie tilted her chin. "I can't take the chance that some beefy football player will knock it down, and I won't allow you to, either. No one should be in physical danger."

The monk kicked the wall. It barely quivered. "A hurricane could blow through and this place would still be standing."

A corner of Lizzie's mouth lifted. "I'll be back on Friday for the final inspection."

As she climbed into her car, Lizzie wondered just exactly when on Friday she could schedule another inspection. *This* was supposed to have been the final inspection. She had other houses, other commissions commanding her attention, including the one at her next destination, a haunted hotel in a nearby tourist ghost town.

Oh, well. Halloween was less than a month away, and the fraternities and sororities wanted to run their haunted house each weekend in October so they could make as much money as possible, a sentiment she heartily endorsed. Besides, her fee would be a percentage of their revenues, since they didn't have enough money up front.

She chuckled to herself. The orange mummy had been extremely effective, catching her unaware. It had been a long time since anything—or anyone—had made her scream.

JARED RUTLEDGE *wanted* to scream. Unfortunately, nothing about the box of body parts was frightening. He was sitting ten feet away and could tell, even in the gloom, that they were fake. Plastic and paint. A cliché.

He rounded a corner. Another coffin, this time with Dracula. Boring.

Ditto for the headless corpse.

Why had he involved himself in this haunted house? Why had he volunteered to design it when he'd promised himself never again?

And blast it, why wasn't anything scary? Had he become so jaded that corpses and assorted unattached limbs had lost their shock value?

"Put your hand in here," instructed his skeleton guide.

Tamping down his impatience, Jared reached through a hole cut in a box and felt a cool, slimy mass.

"Brainssssss," hissed the skeleton.

"Sssssspaghetti," Jared hissed back.

"Perhaps eyeballs are more to your liking," crooned the skeleton.

A sweet smell reached Jared's nose as he squeezed something warm and gooey. "Peeled grapes."

"Are you sure?" the skeleton whispered, a desperate edge on his voice.

Jared examined his damp hand. "Yes."

"Mr. Rutledge, couldn't you at least pretend?"

"I don't want to pretend." Jared searched for something to wipe his hand on. "I want to be convinced. I want to believe."

The skeleton dropped the eyeballs and offered him a paper towel. "Mummy wrappings."

Jared didn't even smile.

"Look," his bony companion began, "try the mad doctor's laboratory. It's next."

With a sense of doom that had nothing to do with what he was about to see, Jared followed the skeleton into the next room.

Predictably it contained a wild-haired doctor wearing a blood-splattered lab coat poised over some unfortunate with two heads. A hunchbacked assistant lurked in the shadows.

Jared shook his head.

"Well, what's the matter?" the skeleton asked defensively.

"It's just not scary enough." Jared rubbed the area between his eyebrows where a headache threatened. The house contained nothing that would inspire anyone to go through, much less pay for the privilege.

"That's 'cause you know what to expect. It's your design."

Jared sighed. Yes, it was his design, or at least the basic structure was. And building this haunted house had been his idea—but not one of his better ones.

It had seemed like a good idea, a fairly simple proposition—design the structure and let the teenagers who volunteered at the physical rehabilitation clinic near his Dallas office build and decorate the inside. They'd have a grand time and the clinic would raise money.

So what had gone wrong? Why did his house lack the sinister spark that drew people?

Jared leaned forward to inspect the mad doctor display and bumped into the operating table. One of the patient's heads jarred loose, rolled off the table and dropped to the floor where it traveled in a drunken spiral until it came to a stop near Jared's feet.

"Here, I'll get that." The skeleton retrieved the head and awkwardly positioned it on the body. "Maybe things'll be scarier when we finish the painting and everybody's dressed up."

"It'll take a lot more than paint."

"More blood?"

Jared was silent for a moment. "No blood."

He'd offered to help because the clinic needed money. And it probably would make some from the patients, their families and friends of the teenagers who were operating the haunted house. Just not enough.

Jared rubbed his forehead again. The headache was now a reality. The staff at the clinic was counting on him. The patients and their families were counting on him. No doubt they'd be thrilled to raise any money at all. He shouldn't spoil it for them.

He smiled, determined to hide his dissatisfaction. "Let's forget scary and look at this from a different perspective. You'll make a lot of kids happy—kids in wheelchairs or on crutches who struggle through the other houses because of the tilted floors and tight corners. Let's not forget, we had to take their physical limitations into consideration."

"Yeah, I know. I just wanted to really scare 'em," the skeleton said, his disappointment obvious.

Jared berated himself, but better disappointment now than later when they counted the money. "It'll still be scary to the younger children."

"You think?"

"Definitely," Jared assured him. "Concentrate on what kind of house this is, instead of what it isn't."

"Okay." The skeleton nodded, slowly at first, then more vigorously. "Yeah. It's not like this is a Wilcox house, or anything."

Jared's smile froze. He never wanted to hear that name again. "No, this isn't a Wilcox house." But when he'd started the design, he'd assumed his house would be just as good, if not better. Wilcox houses must have changed in the last several years.

He wondered if Elizabeth had changed, too.

"We couldn't have afforded her, anyway. She's famous. She does the houses for all the big companies."

"I know." *Believe me, I know.* Every October, the Dallas paper ran a story on Elizabeth Wilcox, the haunted house architect. He never knew when. He only knew that one morning, he'd reach for his coffee, open the paper and there she'd be, staring at him from under a mop of orange hair.

They always printed her picture in color.

She probably dyed her hair.

"If *she'd* designed this house, we'd have made a ton of money."

Jared squeezed his eyes shut as he absorbed the unintentional insult.

"Uh, hey." The skeleton, Danny, ripped off his cape and reached behind his head to remove the mask. "I mean . . . you don't normally do stuff like this."

Conscious of Danny's discomfort, Jared moved toward the exit. "So, have you been through a Wilcox haunted house before?"

"Oh, yeah! It was baaad."

A compliment of the highest order. "What was so . . . bad about it?"

"You never knew what was going to happen. I mean—" Danny began to gesture excitedly "—it was in this little place, but once you got inside you walked and turned and walked—like you'd gone into a huge secret room, or something."

"Lots of steps," Jared murmured to himself. That sounded like Elizabeth. She enjoyed keeping people disoriented, catching them off guard.

"I went through about five times and each time, I saw some more stuff." Danny grinned sheepishly. "Stuff I ran by the other times."

Five times. Repeat business. A big money-maker. And now just the words, "designed by Elizabeth Wilcox" were enough to draw people.

Jared intensely disliked Elizabeth Wilcox.

"And then, once I knew where all the scary places were, you know, I'd take the girls through. I'd be real cool and they'd be screaming and grabbing onto me...."

Danny continued talking, extolling the virtues of the Wilcox house he'd visited. They'd reached the walkway outside the Hanes Memorial Rehabilitation Clinic near downtown Dallas when a van pulled into the drive. As Jared watched, a woman jumped down and opened the back of the van, pulled out a wheelchair and unfolded it. She rolled it around to the side, then maneuvered a young girl out of the van and into the chair.

The girl and her mother were due for a long wait no matter what time their appointment was. The clinic always ran late because it didn't have enough equipment.

As the wheelchair rolled up the entrance ramp, Jared's gaze lingered on the girl's legs, then dropped to his own. His time at the clinic was nearly over, but hers would continue. Years of her young life would be wasted in that crowded waiting room. Wasted because there wasn't enough equipment.

It wasn't fair, and he was determined to raise money for the clinic, even if he had to build a haunted house.

Even if he had to call Elizabeth Wilcox—his ex-wife.

LIZZIE SQUINTED UP at the two-story building one more time, then started her car. The framing was completed on the Haunted Hotel, and now the crew would concentrate on the interior. Everything was right on schedule for the grand opening on Halloween.

She could hardly wait. This was the biggest, most important commission of her career. One that would establish a year-round showcase of her unusual talent—as well as provide a year-round income for the first time. The hotel was in a ghost town being built to bring tourists to an area southwest of Houston. The developers hoped to attract publicity for the town's official spring opening by allowing a sneak peak at the Haunted Hotel on Halloween.

Lizzie planned to supervise this project closely. It was her highest priority, and she wanted it to be perfect.

Thirty minutes later, she breezed past her receptionist's desk in the three-story former residence that now housed her architectural firm. "Any messages, Carleen?"

"Any messages, Carleen," mimicked the plump receptionist. "What do you think? Of course there're messages. There're always messages at this time of year."

Lizzie perched on the corner of Carleen's desk and thumbed through white ghost-shaped pieces of paper. "I remember a time when there weren't messages."

"I don't," Carleen grumbled. "I've had that phone stuck in my ear all day." She glared at the telephone, which promptly warbled. "Great. Now when am I supposed to put up the Halloween decorations?"

Lizzie laughed and slid off the desk. "If that's for me, I'll take it in my office."

Carleen nodded, answered the phone and put the caller on hold. "Surprise. It's for you."

Having anticipated that the call would be, Lizzie was already walking toward her office. She paused in the doorway, admiring the spacious, light-drenched room and was filled with a sense of well-being. She was busy, but happy. How many other people really liked their jobs?

Lizzie approached her desk and dragged the phone across it, so she could sit on the window ledge and gaze outside while she talked. She loved autumn, even though Houston autumns weren't the crisp, bright-leafed autumns of her childhood.

And she loved October. Wonderful things happened in October.

"Hello," she said brightly, her happiness apparent in her voice.

"Elizabeth?"

The well-bred masculine tones shattered Lizzie's good mood.

"Yes," she managed, with the last breath of air left in her lungs.

"Elizabeth, it's Jared."

She knew that. She'd known his voice instantly.

What she didn't know was why he was calling her after three years. She remembered clearly her last words to him: *If you change your mind, call me.* Well, the statute of limitations had run out on changes of mind.

"Jared Rutledge," he elaborated with irritation, obviously taking her silence for nonrecognition.

"Hello, Jared." *Hello Jared?* She'd waited over three years for him to call and the best she could come up with was hello, Jared.

"How have you been, Elizabeth?"

"Fine." What a silly conversation this was. But still, terribly correct and polite. Just like all their conversations during the ugly time they'd met at lawyers' offices to dissolve their business.

And their marriage.

It was her turn to ask a question. She wasn't going to, because the only one she wanted to ask was why he'd called. But his silence chided her. She was supposed to say something. "How are your parents?"

"They're well," he replied.

Jared's parents lived in Sweetwater, a country-club community south of Houston. He was probably in town visiting them. She almost asked, except it wasn't her turn.

"I've been hearing quite a bit about your...work."

The hesitation was slight, but Lizzie had been listening carefully. She could hear the effort Jared made to be conciliatory, elevating her designs to the status of "work."

Jared had always looked down his very patrician nose at her haunted house designs.

And, eventually, he'd looked down his nose at her.

She pushed away the hurtful memories. So he'd been hearing about her. "I've been interviewed by a lot of reporters lately. Haunted houses are seasonal, and this *is* my busiest time of year." Maybe he'd take the hint and get to the point of his phone call.

"Yes." He cleared his throat. "I've designed a haunted house—"

"*You?*" Lizzie exploded in a laugh. "I thought you never wanted anything to do with haunted houses again." Or anyone who designed them.

"Haunted houses have their place. I chose not to make them my life's calling."

And Lizzie had. She heard the implied criticism and bristled.

Jared continued, "I've become associated with a physical therapy clinic here in Dallas, and I wanted to help them raise money. A haunted house seemed like the best way to do that."

"Because you thought it would be easy," Lizzie scoffed.

There was a rebuking pause. "As I recall, the houses we built together in college weren't difficult," he said evenly.

"That was a long time ago." They'd raised more money than any other project in the history of the school. She and Jared had won an award. She wondered where the plaque was now.

"We worked well together didn't we, Elizabeth?"

Lizzie gripped the telephone receiver. She recognized that honeyed tone in Jared's voice. He used it when he wanted something from her. She'd always found it difficult to refuse without sounding petty and unreasonable. "What do you want?"

He chuckled, seemingly unperturbed that his favorite form of manipulation was no longer effective. "I want you to help me build the house."

Oh, he did, did he? "Why?"

"It's what you do for a living, isn't it?"

"Yes, it is. I meant, why me?"

"You're supposed to be the best."

If not for the "supposed to" Jared had inserted, Lizzie would have been flattered. She said nothing.

The silence stretched. "Am I supposed to beg now?" Disdain filled his voice.

It didn't bother her. She'd heard disdain in his voice before. Frequently. "Depends on how desperate you are."

She'd expected that to end their conversation. To her surprise, Jared responded quietly. "This project is important to me and some special people who're depending on me. I want it to succeed." She heard him take a deep breath, as if forcing himself to continue. "Would you come take a look at it?"

"You want *me* to come to Dallas?" she asked in amazement.

"Yes. And after you see the house, you can make some suggestions or redo the design."

"Jared!" Lizzie was nearly speechless. "You don't know what you're asking."

"It's for a good cause—"

"They're all good causes—"

"Okay. How about if I give you the dimensions now, and then you jot down a few ideas and fax them to me?"

"I don't just churn out designs. I spend at least ten to fourteen days on them!" Nothing infuriated Lizzie more than someone belittling her career. "My houses take two to three months to build. This is the first of October. You don't have time to build a house this year. If you want to commission a design for next year, I'll schedule you in."

"Then come to Dallas and tell me how to fix this one." He sounded like the Jared of old. The persuasive and determined Jared who always had an answer to every objection. Nothing would *dare* go wrong with Jared at the helm.

But she couldn't go to Dallas. Oh, she wanted to. She wanted to gloat. She wanted to show him how successful she'd become. If only he'd called, say, in March. But he hadn't. "I don't have time."

"For this project or for me?"

That wasn't fair. "For *anyone.*"

"Flights leave Houston for Dallas every half hour." Jared never gave up. "You could fly up in the morning, look at the site and be back in your office after lunch."

How like him to assume she had entire half days free. "This is my busiest time of the year," she reiterated. "Every minute is booked from now until after Halloween. I can't."

"Please." His voice was gruff.

"Jared . . ." Lizzie felt herself weaken, despite all the years of telling herself she was better off without him.

"For the kids, then. Handicapped children, Elizabeth."

Lizzie exhaled sharply. "You're pulling all the strings, aren't you?"

"Whatever it takes."

And it didn't used to take much, she remembered. She and Jared had been a team—publicly and privately.

But that was ancient history. "I realize you think I'm exacting some sort of petty revenge by refusing to help, but I'm not. I simply don't have the time."

He obviously didn't believe her. "I'll pay you."

He meant to shame her, but he didn't. "*If* I had the time, I'd expect to be paid. This is how I make my living."

"Then is business so good you can afford to turn down a fee because you're bitter?"

"Actually, it is." And she was delighted to say so. "Now goodbye, Jared."

"Elizabeth . . . wait. Don't hang up. Please."

If he'd commanded her not to hang up, she would have slammed down the phone. But she couldn't resist his quiet plea.

Only a few moments ticked by before her surrender. "Tell me about the house." It was a mistake and she knew it.

Well, nobody was perfect.

He immediately launched into a description. "This house has some special constraints. It must be completely wheelchair accessible. That means no bumpy floors or obstructions can contribute to the atmosphere."

"All my designs are wheelchair accessible," Lizzie informed him with satisfaction. She'd designed them that way even before it was mandatory.

"But being accessible and being enjoyable are entirely different!" Jared snapped. "Giving those kids a good time is as important to me as raising the money. I tried lowering the scary sights to wheelchair level. And rather than a lot of narrow corridors, I built a series of connecting rooms, but the house isn't effective."

"Have you blocked out all the lights?"

"Yes."

"Tell me what I'd see if I went through."

"You'd be guided by a skeleton." Using a guide was his first mistake, Lizzie thought. "First, there's a crypt, then a dungeon, Dracula's coffin, the mad doctor's lab . . ."

Lizzie closed her eyes as Jared described his haunted house. There was not one original idea or startle. It was extremely tame by haunted house standards, and Lizzie knew massive modifications would be required if he hoped to compete with the professional houses—including two of her designs—operating in the Dallas area this Halloween.

The public had become much more sophisticated since the early days of her business. On the other hand, Jared had indicated that the house was primarily for wheelchairs. An interesting angle. She would've enjoyed the challenge.

But not this year. "I'm sure the house will be fine, Jared."

"No, it isn't fine!" he lashed out. "If I thought it was fine, I wouldn't be talking to you now!"

"I see."

"Elizabeth—"

"Jared Rutledge is sacrificing himself for a greater good. How noble of you to stoop to designing frivolous structures, Jared."

Lizzie found a particular pleasure in throwing Jared's own words back at him. *I'd rather starve than design frivolous structures for a living,* he'd said. And she'd said, *if you change your mind, call me.*

He never had. Until today.

"I suppose I deserved that."

"Yes, you did."

"I apologize if I hurt you."

"*If* you hurt me?" *Why* had she said that? Lizzie held her breath, wishing she could take back her words.

"You must despise me, maybe even hate me." He sounded thoughtful.

Lizzie's laugh was strained. Jared was uncomfortably close to the truth. "I hardly give you a thought."

He ignored her. "I'll bet you've been dying for a chance to show me how successful you've become."

Even though she was alone in her office, Lizzie felt her face heat in a blush of embarrassment. "Nonsense."

"Think, Elizabeth. You'd be in charge. You could boss me around and make my life miserable." His voice took on that familiar honeyed resonance. "Here's your chance—"

"Jared, I'm much too busy to continue this absurd conversation—"

"Maybe the only chance you'll ever get. Are you woman enough to take it?"

CHAPTER TWO

ONLY A FOOL WOULD FALL for such an obvious ploy.

So why was Lizzie flying to Dallas?

She knew Jared had to be desperate to have called her. But had she let him wallow in his desperation? Had she told him, "Tough luck, buster?"

No, like a wimp, she'd fallen for his silver-tongued manipulations. She was more marshmallow than architect.

Not only had she told Jared she'd take a look at his haunted house, which was bad enough, but she'd also told him she'd come today—that was where the marshmallow part came in.

Oh, he'd been absolutely right in everything he'd said. She *did* want to sashay over to his site, wave a magic wand and solve his problems, thus leaving him forever in her debt. And then she planned to remind him of it—frequently.

Lizzie adjusted the miniblinds at her bedroom window to let in the morning light and wandered over to her closet.

She wanted to gloat. She wanted an apology for the way he'd sneered at her work. She wanted to hear him say, "Elizabeth, I was wrong and you were right."

She wanted his approval.

And that bothered her.

His opinion had mattered to her for so long, deferring to it had become a bad habit. What difference should Jared Rutledge's opinions about anything make to her?

He was nothing to her now. She rarely thought about him.

Lizzie flipped through her clothes. If she was going to be a marshmallow, she was going to be a professional marshmallow. Then she caught herself rejecting clothes based on whether or not Jared would approve of them. Gritting her teeth, she blindly reached for anything vaguely appropriate.

Happily, the pumpkin-colored city shorts outfit she grabbed was perfect. She adored fall colors and enjoyed wearing the golds and oranges and cinnamons and browns and forest greens that set off her carroty red hair.

As she flung the suit on the bed, her eye caught the glowing numerals of her digital clock.

She was late. Any moment now, Carleen's footsteps would sound on the stairs. If Lizzie wasn't downstairs by eight-thirty in the morning, Carleen had instructions to wake her up.

Lizzie lived in an airy apartment on the third floor of the building housing her firm. It was not uncommon for her to toil long into the night and fall asleep sprawled on the pillowed couch.

Last night, she'd done precisely that. In order to clear the morning for Jared, she'd fine-tuned designs and composed a list of instructions for Carleen.

"Lizzie, are you awake?" Carleen, right on schedule.

"Coming!" Lizzie called.

"You've got to see what I bought," Carleen continued talking through the closed door, bursting inside when Lizzie finally opened it. "Look!"

"A Halloween wreath." Lizzie examined the straw circle decorated with ghosts, bats, witches, skeletons and pumpkins. Spiders dangled below and a yellow moon rose above. "This is perfect for the front door."

"Sure beats Indian corn." Carleen beamed. After a moment, Lizzie realized she was supposed to notice something else. Carleen gently shook her head, sending white ghost earrings swaying.

"Those are great." Lizzie grinned, tweaking an earring with her finger.

"Glad you like them." Carleen handed Lizzie a small white box. "I bought a pair for you, too."

"Thanks. You may be the only person who likes Halloween more than I do." Lizzie stood in front of the mirror over her fireplace mantel and clipped on the ghost earrings.

Carleen held her wreath up against Lizzie's door and studied the effect. "Why can't we decorate three months early for Halloween the way stores do for Christmas?"

"I don't know...Halloween decorations in August?" Lizzie held her hair back and shook her head. The lightweight ghosts danced and bobbed. "Tell you what, next year I'll let you put up the decorations in the last week of September."

"Hooray!" Carleen turned to go. "I'll write a note on the calendar and try to think up another bribe by then."

Lizzie laughed as the door closed behind her effervescent secretary.

She admired her ghost earrings for a while longer, then reluctantly removed them. Today was not the day for silly earrings. Not if she wanted Jared to take her seriously.

And she did. She might as well admit it and stop feeling guilty about wanting him to see her as a success. He'd never thought she could support herself designing haunted houses. He'd thought she would fail. She hadn't.

Lizzie dressed quickly, accessorizing the suit with tasteful gold earrings and plain black sneakers, rather than the ones sporting appliquéd pumpkins. She examined herself in the bathroom's full-length mirror. The city shorts were fashionable and practical. When she climbed around construction sites, she didn't wear dresses and it was too hot for pants.

But her hair was all wrong. It was naturally curly and usually did whatever it wanted in the Houston humidity. Today her hair was particularly wild and unruly. Lizzie gathered it into a bunch and clipped it back with a tortoise shell barrette.

My, didn't she look dowdy. Jared would approve. Jared liked dowdiness in businesswomen. He thought the more dowdy they were, the more successful they were, presumably because they didn't take time away from their businesses to shop for clothes.

After a short inner debate, Lizzie fastened a gold house pin to her lapel. At least it would appear to be a house pin to the casual observer. Any female architect might wear such a pin. Unique, but tasteful. In fact, no one would notice the bats or the ghosts or the scraggly tree branches unless they spent a great deal of time staring at her left breast.

And so what if Jared *did* notice the pin?

She grinned. She could have worn her skull with the blinking red eyes.

Carleen wasn't at her desk when Lizzie trotted down the stairs. She found her outside, putting ghost and pumpkin lights in the bushes.

"Where are you going?" Carleen asked.

"Dallas," Lizzie answered breezily.

"Not today you're not. At ten o'clock, you're meeting with the Pearland Civic Committee, and at noon, you promised those college kids you'd be back for a final inspection of their Shrieks by Greeks house." Carleen never confused the frivolous with the practical.

Lizzie felt guilty. "Please reschedule the Civic people. You can fax them the preliminary sketches I drew last night. If they have technical questions, they can ask Edward." Edward was her assistant, a recent graduate apprenticing with her until he passed his licensing exam.

"They didn't hire Edward. They hired you."

"They hired Elizabeth Wilcox Architects, with an 's.' I did the sketches, and I'll do the design. Just not the meeting today."

Carleen stopped stringing lights and looked at her. "And the college kids?"

Lizzie fingered one of the lights. "Tell them I'll come by later this afternoon."

"So you'll be returning today."

Lizzie nodded.

Carleen clicked her tongue. "I'll check the calendar and see when you can fit in the Civic Committee."

Feeling like a chastened schoolgirl, Lizzie followed her secretary inside.

"Let's see...." Carleen put on her reading glasses and flipped through the scheduling calendar.

Lizzie couldn't look.

"Hmm." Carleen peered over the tops of her glasses, then turned the book around so it faced Lizzie. "You pick a time."

Every block of time contained a scribbled note.

"What's Edward's calendar like?"

"Almost as bad."

Lizzie glanced at her watch and bit her lip. "I've got to get to the airport or I'm going to blow the whole day." She sighed, staring at her packed calendar. "See what you can reschedule for four o'clock on."

Carleen's mouth was set in a disapproving line as she turned the calendar back around. "You aren't scheduled to visit Dallas until the week after next. Trouble with the Richardson Mall project?"

"No." Lizzie checked the clasps on her briefcase to avoid Carleen's speculative gaze.

"Where can you be reached?"

"Uh, through Rutledge Architects."

"You're kidding."

"No." Lizzie wished she'd never confided in Carleen. But when the motherly Carleen had wanted to know why Lizzie never accepted dates, Lizzie had told her all about Jared—in watery detail.

"Would this be the same Rutledge who was your partner?"

"The very one."

"The man to whom you were married for four years?"

"Four and a half." Involuntarily, Lizzie rubbed her bare ring finger.

"The Jared Rutledge you cried over when you thought I wasn't looking?"

"Go finish stringing your lights," Lizzie mumbled.

"I'd like to string *his* lights," was Carleen's spirited reply.

Lizzie sent a look of exasperated affection toward her secretary. "It's okay, Carleen. He needs my help."

"For what?"

"He's building a haunted house."

"So tell him to get in line and no cuts." Her secretary scanned the appointment book. "Here. You've got an opening in January."

"I want to go today and get it over with." Lizzie hoisted her briefcase and started for the door. "Besides, I know how much it annoyed him to have to call me. He must be in a real fix."

"Be careful," Carleen warned. "You act jumpier than a frog in a hot skillet."

Lizzie chuckled. "Don't worry, Carleen. This is just another consultation. I resolved my feelings for Jared long ago."

SHE LIED.

She hadn't resolved anything. Didn't she secretly hope Jared was using the haunted house as an excuse to see her again? As a way of apologizing for ridiculing her occupation?

Lizzie spent the entire one-hour flight to Dallas lost in a nostalgic fog.

Jared, with his lethal smile, his intensity and his enthusiasm for their projects. The way he had taken her innovative ideas and turned them into viable designs. The fire in his eyes as they'd planned their life together. Late nights spent studying. The struggles they'd shared setting up their business.

These were all feelings she tried to squash by dredging up memories of the bitter quarrels and hurtful insults they'd flung at each other.

Still, as the plane landed, she had to wipe her palms on the seat. Her heart pounded and her stomach churned with the anticipation of seeing him again.

Deliberately waiting to be the last one off the plane, she stepped out of the jetway and scanned the crowd for Jared's tall figure.

But Jared wasn't there. When she didn't see him she hesitated, searching for anyone who might be looking for her. She should be expected; she'd called his office from the airport in Houston and told them what flight she'd be on.

It was soon obvious that no one was meeting her. Miffed, she called Jared's office again. They informed her that he was already at the site.

How imperious. How arrogant. How typical. By now, Lizzie was angrier with herself than she was with Jared. *He'd* asked for *her* help, yet here she was, dropping everything at his convenience. He might have shown some consideration or a little gratitude.

She had to rent a car. The Dallas-Fort Worth airport was miles from anything and a fortune in cab fare.

Grumbling during the entire drive to the Hanes Memorial Haunted House, she was surprised to feel her palms dampen again as she neared the building site.

Get a grip, she commanded herself as she turned into the clinic's parking lot. Once was enough for the sweaty palms and queasy stomach drill.

The Hanes Memorial Rehabilitation Clinic wasn't very big. They didn't look as if they could afford much in the way of haunted houses.

If done correctly haunted houses were great money-makers, but they required an initial investment of materials and labor that could run to thousands of dollars.

Even so, it was rather small potatoes for Jared.

No, she was being unfair. The Jared she'd gone to school with had felt no job was too small to be designed well.

But the Jared she'd gone to school with had grown into the life-is-too-serious-to-have-fun Jared she'd left.

Which Jared had called her two days ago?

Lizzie parked her car, searching for any Jared at all.

The site was deserted, except for two vans parked outside the clinic.

Hanes Memorial was in a medical office park with several freestanding buildings clustered around beautifully landscaped grounds that gleamed in the bright sunlight.

The haunted house, also freestanding, was an eyesore, just as it should be. It was easily accessible and near a busy intersection, allowing it plenty of exposure.

Lizzie had to give Jared some credit for a good location, much as she didn't want to. At least he hadn't forgotten everything they'd learned together.

She could hear pounding from inside the house and picked her way over discarded lumber. The hammering continued. She inhaled, ready to call out and noted the distinctive odor of fire-retardant paint. Good.

"Hello, Elizabeth."

She jumped. *Jared*.

His voice came from behind her. She turned, looking up, her neck muscles instantly remembering how far back she had to tilt her head to meet his eyes.

To meet his lips.

"Hello, Jar—"

She faltered when her gaze was drawn down to the man sitting before her.

The man sitting in a wheelchair.

Lizzie gasped and stared. She felt the blood rush from her head, leaving her woozy.

"Jared," she whispered. "Why didn't you tell me?" Dropping her briefcase, she sank to her knees, clutching the arm of the wheelchair. Tears filled her eyes. No wonder he hadn't met her at the airport.

"Elizabeth...no. Don't cry. You don't understand." She heard him swear softly. "This isn't what you think."

She felt his hands on her shoulders as his image blurred. Jared, *her* Jared had been hurt. He'd needed her and she hadn't been there for him.

"What's there to think?" she choked, the tears spilling out. She didn't care that crying made her freckled face blotchy. "You're in a wheelchair!"

"Not for long." He shook her shoulder. "Elizabeth..."

He was being so brave. She gazed into his coffee-colored eyes, shaded by heavy black brows. A dry breeze ruffled the layers of his hair, still the same rich sable. His jaw was as chiseled as ever, and his chin, which had a tendency to jut when he was being obstinate, was still as prominent.

"How did it hap—pen?" Her voice broke.

One long-fingered hand squeezed hers, his thumb moving soothingly across her knuckles. "An accident. Listen to me," he commanded with the beginnings of irritation. "It's only temporary. I'll recover. I'm going to walk again."

Temporary? Recover? "You will?" Lizzie sniffed. "Really?" It would be just like Jared to tell her that so she wouldn't worry about him. Dear Jared.

"*Really,*" he said in his you're-being-overdramatic-again voice.

"Oh."

A corner of his mouth slanted upward. "Don't sound so disappointed."

She snatched her hand away. "I'm not." But she was rather chagrined to find herself blubbering over a minor injury. "I'm delighted." She gave a delighted little laugh to prove it. "It was the . . . the shock."

And Jared in a wheelchair wasn't the only shock, a shaky Lizzie discovered as she stood. Her knees felt damp. She looked down and saw they were coated with dirt. Brushing off the moist earth gave her a chance to recover from the stunning realization that besides not having resolved her feelings for Jared, she still cared for him.

Deeply.

Too deeply.

Furthermore, she knew her emotions had gone sailing across her face for him to read. Now *he'd* gloat. "You might have warned me, that's all."

"It didn't occur to me to mention my temporary confinement to a wheelchair. I forgot you didn't know." His gaze moved over her, stopping somewhere, she judged, in the area of her left breast. Lizzie hoped her pounding heart wasn't visible beneath the pin.

She'd intended to remain coolly remote. Purely professional. But how could she act remote after practically fainting at his feet?

Lizzie picked up her briefcase and rubbed off the dirt clinging to the bottom. She'd have to treat him like an old, dear friend, who happened to be an ex-husband. Someone she'd outgrown, but nonetheless thought of fondly—when she thought of him at all.

"Jared, dear, how *have* you been other than.. ?" Lizzie waved vaguely.

"Other than shattering my ankle and living in this wheeled prison for five weeks?" He sounded testy.

"Does it hurt?"

"Of course, it hurts!"

He was understandably cranky. She'd forgive him. "Poor Jared."

"Would you quit saying my name like I'm the family pet?"

"Yes, Jared." Lizzie patted him on the head. They were back to badgering one another. She understood badgering. She excelled at badgering.

Jared gave her a look that slowly melted into the wintry smile. "Elizabeth, how *have* I managed without you?"

"Not at all well." She reached out and snapped his suspenders. "You look as if you need somebody to loosen you up."

Something flashed in his eyes, then his smile turned mocking. "And you think Frizzy Lizzie, the Scream Queen, is the perfect candidate?"

"Maybe." She swallowed back a biting retort. Unfortunately, badgering had a tendency to degenerate into quarreling. And there was no need to quarrel just because he'd used her old nickname. He'd probably forgotten how much she hated it. However, it was obviously up to her to set the professional standards during this meeting. "Shall we inspect your haunted house?"

He gestured toward the doorway. "This house is geared for people in wheelchairs, you remember."

"I remember." Lizzie stepped into a sizable room. Wasted space, she thought immediately. "Where's your scare by the entrance?"

"There isn't one. We don't want to give anything away to the people waiting outside."

"That's okay. Your patrons should be thrown off balance right away. Show them you mean business." She walked on. "What happens next?"

Jared rolled over to a coffin. "We let them look in this." He lifted the lid and showed a shrouded skeleton. "While their attention is on the skeleton in this coffin, another skeleton jumps out and scares them."

"From where?"

Jared pointed to a corridor ahead of them.

Lizzie shook her head. "You've got to scare forward. If the skeleton enters from this direction, they'll run—roll—back toward the entrance and jam up with the next group."

Jared considered her words. "Then we won't allow the next group in until this one leaves the room."

Lizzie set her briefcase on the skeleton's coffin and removed some paper. "You'll only serve half as many people that way. Let's build a wall here—" she gestured toward the doorway "—and the skeleton can jump from behind there. That way, you'll scare the group out of this room faster, and you can let in the next bunch."

"Perfect," Jared agreed. "I don't know why I didn't think of that."

His compliment made her heart skitter. "Because you don't spend all year studying and building haunted houses." Maybe now, he'd understand some of what went into one of her designs.

"Thank heaven for that!" Jared wheeled over to examine her sketch.

Lizzie felt the same old hurt, but held her tongue. He probably didn't even realize he'd insulted her. She'd ignore it because when he thought back on this consultation, she wanted him to remember how professional and competent she'd acted.

He watched as she drew. "I knew it would only take you a few minutes to get this place into shape."

"Maybe a bit longer than that," she murmured and sensed his thoughtful scrutiny of her.

"You know, you really are talented." His voice was warmly sincere.

Happiness bubbled within her. She stopped drawing to gaze down at him. He wore the crooked smile that had always made her toes curl.

She should look away. It wasn't a good idea to let him see how much she still cared. "Thank you," she said softly.

"Elizabeth—" he leaned forward, an intent expression on his face "—why haven't you tried to design something really important?"

A deadly quiet fell between them.

The nostalgia, which had haunted her ever since his call, dissipated. "Really important?"

"I know you could," he insisted, "if you'd only try."

"I thought *this*—" Lizzie gestured around her "—was important. So important that you asked me to drop everything to come here."

Jared made an exasperated sound. "You know what I mean."

"Yes." She stared at him for a long moment. "I think I do."

He despised her work. And he'd never reverse his opinion. She remembered his contempt for her and her designs at the end of their marriage.

She also remembered how she'd attempted to change herself. How she'd always played peacemaker in their relationship.

Even today, she'd held her tongue, shrugged off remarks and gritted her teeth until her jaw ached.

What was she doing here? What was the matter with her? She didn't have to tolerate his cutting remarks in order to preserve their marriage. There was no longer a marriage to preserve.

She didn't need this. She certainly didn't need him. *She* had flown to Dallas. *She* had canceled appointments. If she left now, she could still meet with the college kids at noon and stop by the Haunted Hotel, too.

All in all, Lizzie felt she could allow herself the luxury of a grand exit.

She shoved her sketches into her briefcase. Without a word, without a flounce, without a backward glance, Lizzie, consciously professional, strode out the front door of the Hanes Memorial Haunted House and headed toward her rental car.

"Elizabeth?" Jared called from inside.

She unlocked the car.

"Elizabeth, what are you doing?" He was at the entrance now.

She opened the door, tossed her briefcase inside and climbed in after it.

"Elizabeth!" he roared.

She slammed the door, then unfastened her tortoiseshell barrette, freeing her hair.

"Elizabeth?" Muffled.

She cranked the ignition and shook out her hair, running her fingers through it, encouraging it to fluff.

"*E-liiizzz-a-beeeth!*"

Lizzie smiled and adjusted her rearview mirror so she could see Jared's face.

Then she drove off.

CHAPTER THREE

JARED SLAPPED THE ARMS of his wheelchair and bit back a curse. Still the same temperamental Elizabeth, who considered her bizarre designs high art.

Once, her antics had been refreshingly appealing. By the end of their marriage, they'd become tiresomely irritating. He'd hoped she might have matured. But no, she continued to indulge in dramatic tantrums and grand exits.

This time he couldn't run after her.

The last time he *hadn't* run after her.

And she hadn't come back. He had no doubt she wouldn't come back this time, either.

He wasn't entirely sure what had set her off but suspected it was his remark about her designing something important. He'd meant to be complimentary. She *was* quick and talented, and it had always bothered him that she hadn't tackled a major commission.

He should've left the subject alone. He as good as accused her of wasting her talent drawing junk. But that's what she did. Throwaway designs. Nothing that would last. Nothing she could look back on years from now and say proudly, "I designed that."

Maybe that didn't bother her. And it shouldn't bother him.

Jared ran his fingers through his hair. Okay, he shouldn't have criticized her. But why couldn't she have just said, "Jared, if I want to design junk, I'll design junk."

Because it wasn't dramatic enough.

"Is she here yet?" Danny's voice sounded behind him.

Jared gazed at the empty spot where Elizabeth's car had been parked. "Here and gone."

"Already?"

Jared exhaled through gritted teeth.

"Did she even look at the house?" Danny asked, perplexed. "Will she help us?"

She might if Jared groveled. Elizabeth enjoyed creative groveling. "I don't know." He rolled himself through the doorway.

Danny followed him outside. "What happened?"

"An old disagreement got in the way."

"Huh?"

Jared glanced over his shoulder. "She's my ex-wife."

"Wow." Danny regarded him with awe. "You were *married* to her? Then how come you don't design haunted houses like she does?"

A corner of Jared's mouth tilted upward. "*That* was the old disagreement."

"Oh." Danny kicked at a piece of board. "I guess that's that then."

Jared hated disappointing him. "Elizabeth's difficult to get along with," he said. "When something sets her off, she just explodes. For instance, I had this habit of tapping my pencil when I concentrated. I wasn't aware of it. Apparently, the noise irritated her. Instead of calmly drawing my attention to it, one evening she let out a blood-chilling shriek, ran over to my desk, snapped all my pencils in half and then flung the pieces all over the room." Actually the incident was rather funny, now that he thought about it.

"Man, that's a bad scene."

Jared shrugged. "That's Elizabeth. She lets her anger build until—pow." He swept his arms wide. "You never know what or when." A wry smile touched his lips. "If you're an artist, it's called being temperamental."

"Sounds like my sister having a tantrum."

"It sounds exactly like it," Jared agreed with a laugh.

Danny nudged the wood scraps into a pile. "What about our house? Are you going to call her again?"

Good question. Jared didn't know the answer.

For years, he'd tolerated Elizabeth's moodiness and her roller coaster emotions. It had been exhausting.

But he'd never been bored. In fact, right now, he felt more alive than he had since their divorce.

He felt invigorated.

He felt guilty.

Jared had never expected to see the agonized expression in Elizabeth's eyes at the sight of him in a wheelchair. It had been thoughtless of him not to warn her. Her reaction had stunned him. He'd known, right then, that she still had feelings for him.

And, so help him, he still had feelings for her.

The smart thing would be to forget he ever knew her.

"TELL HIM TO MAKE an appointment."

"He only wants to talk to you. He seems like such a nice man."

Lizzie narrowed her eyes. Carleen had gone over to the enemy. "Of course, he seems that way. But he isn't. He's pigheaded and arrogant." She glared at Carleen, who tried to glare back.

Unfortunately, Carleen wore her rhinestone cat eye-glasses, so thanks to the tails dangling on either side of her face, she didn't have the intimidating effect Lizzie was sure she wanted.

"But Lizzie—"

"But Lizzie, nothing. You only like him because he sent that stupid balloon."

The balloon gesture was rather whimsical for Jared.

"It's very clever." Carleen crept closer to the offending balloon, which drifted about the office, annoying Lizzie to no end. She'd pop the thing, but she knew Carleen would be devastated.

It was a huge Mylar pumpkin filled with helium. Tissue paper arms and legs dangled from it, weighing it down just enough so that it hovered and drifted four feet off the ground. Jared had written "I'm sorry," next to its leering grin.

Carleen amused herself by fanning the balloon down the hall until it bounced into Lizzie's office—several irksome times a day.

"He *does* sound sorry. And it wasn't *only* the balloon."

"What else did he send?" Lizzie asked suspiciously.

Carleen glanced sideways and ducked her head guiltily. Lizzie followed her gaze to an orange foil box. "Not the white chocolate ghosts." Ugh. She'd actually eaten some of those.

Carleen nodded. "And the marshmallow pumpkins."

"You're welcome to them." Lizzie studied the area around the reception desk. A kitchen witch on a broomstick hung over the file cabinet. Pointing, she raised her eyebrows.

Carleen shrugged, palms upward.

Lizzie rolled her eyes. "How humiliating. My secretary can be bribed."

"But I don't come cheap." The phone rang again. "It's probably Jared," Carleen said. "He usually calls about this time. And he'll just want to talk to you."

"Then he can make an appointment!"

And Jared made an appointment. Carleen was quick to find an opening, complaining about Lizzie's thoughtlessness in forcing that "nice man" to travel with a wheelchair.

The morning of Jared's appointment, Lizzie took no special care in dressing. She refused to alter her natural style simply because he was coming. She dressed in black, because she felt like it, and tried to pretend this was just another workday.

But of course it wasn't just another workday.

Thus, she knew the exact moment Jared arrived because she'd been watching out her window. She wanted to see his reaction when he saw her office.

She adored the old house and had poured herself into the remodeling. The building was located in a neighborhood with other renovated homes and small businesses, and the branches of huge live oaks formed a deep green canopy over the street.

Unfortunately, the streets and curbs had been built at a time when cars were higher off the ground. Jared had to pull into the driveway so he could roll out of the van. Lizzie winced when she saw him struggle to maneuver his chair over the flagstones leading to her entrance.

She had thought the flagstones pretty, and they were. But there was nothing pretty about Jared's struggle. She started for the door to help, then stopped. The independent Jared wouldn't appreciate it.

Lizzie could hear Carleen clucking and remembered the two low steps in front of her door. She hadn't realized they'd present a problem.

She immediately made a note to have ramps installed. It didn't matter that Jared would soon be out of his chair. What if she had other clients in wheelchairs? She was appalled that it had taken this to enlighten her.

"Elizabeth?" Jared appeared in the doorway. "Your secretary sent me on back."

"Come in." Lizzie noted the sheen of perspiration on his forehead and his slightly flushed face. The color looked good on him. Healthy. When they'd been married, Lizzie had seen to it that Jared exercised and spent time outdoors. He had a tendency to work too hard.

She wondered if he . . . no. Jared's work habits were no longer any concern of hers.

Jared rolled through the doorway, nicking the paint. He winced. "I'm sorry. I don't know if I'll ever get the knack of this thing."

"It's all right. I apologize for not having a ramp. I'll get one immediately." Lizzie heard herself babbling and tried to slow down. "The steps outside were so small, I didn't realize they'd be a problem for people in wheelchairs."

Jared held up a hand. "Believe me, this experience has made me aware of how difficult it is for those in wheelchairs to get around."

"You know, I've heard friends with children in strollers complain, too."

They smiled at each other. How well they were getting along, Lizzie thought. As long as they didn't talk about their jobs—or each other.

SO FAR, SO GOOD, Jared thought. She hadn't thrown him out, but after all, he did have an appointment. Luckily, she had a secretary with a sweet tooth.

Elizabeth's office was big, probably the largest in the entire building. The room was spacious and decorated with surprisingly good taste, considering her penchant for ethnic eccentricities. Framed pictures of ramshackle buildings adorned her walls. Her haunted houses. She could be forgiven for displaying them.

Elizabeth had done well. He was genuinely pleased for her, though she'd never believe him if he told her.

He rolled over to her desk, watching her watch him. Her feet, encased in red tennis shoes with black beading, twitched. Elizabeth was nervous. Good. He needed her help and wasn't above exploiting her weaknesses to get it.

"How did you hurt yourself?" she asked.

He thought he'd told her. "On a site inspection. We'd been having trouble with a contractor substituting substandard grades of materials. Unfortunately, I lost my temper and chose to demonstrate the hazards of such substitutions on the second story of a building."

Her eyes widened. He'd forgotten how blue they were. "You fell?"

Jared nodded ruefully. "And caught my foot on the way down. If I hadn't torn it up so much, I could have had a walking cast right away."

"I'm sorry." Elizabeth did look genuinely sorry. In fact, she looked quite appealing right now, in spite of the hideous skull with the flashing eyes she wore pinned to her lapel. Her hair caught the morning sunlight in flaming corkscrews that curled well below her shoulders.

Liz, Liz, freckles and frizz. He remembered how they'd made fun of her at their school's annual Spring Fling. Of course the graduating seniors made fun of everybody, but Elizabeth hadn't been amused. The next day, she'd bought a chemical straightener and applied it to her hair—with disastrous results.

What hadn't broken off had to be cropped close to her scalp, leaving her with a halo of wavy wisps and a sudden penchant for scarves.

Jared had found her sobbing in her sorority house when they were supposed to be at their graduation ceremony.

And at approximately the same time they should have been walking across the stage to receive their diplomas, Jared Rutledge had proposed to Elizabeth Wilcox.

"WHAT ARE YOU GRINNING at?" Lizzie demanded, uncomfortable with the expression on Jared's face.

"Memories."

He looked at her a moment longer, then gestured around the room. "You've done well, I see. How much of the building do you lease?"

"The whole thing. I own it." *Take that, Jared.*

"Congratulations." Jared's gaze dropped to the cardboard tube in his lap.

Lizzie found that gloating wasn't very satisfying.

"Elizabeth, I want to collaborate with you on this project, if you're willing."

"I'm willing, *if* you can refrain from insulting me."

"I'll agree, *if* you'll stop indulging in childish tantrums."

"Childish tantrums?"

"Yes—like the other day when you ran off."

Lizzie's toes curled. She stood and walked around her desk, then leaning against it, she crossed her arms. It was rude to tower over Jared, but she didn't care. She took a deep breath. "I left because I didn't have to stay."

"What?" He seemed genuinely perplexed.

"*I* canceled appointments, *I* gave up my time to travel to Dallas. You insulted me—the way you always do. Once, I would've tried to ignore it, not let it bother me . . . anything to preserve our business, our marriage. But there's no business and no marriage to preserve anymore. I don't have to tolerate your verbal abuse—"

"*Verbal abuse?*" Jared's dark brows drew together in a thick ominous line.

"—and I won't."

She watched as he struggled with his anger. It was always like this when they argued. Why didn't he just let it out? Yell? Throw something?

"We were very young, Elizabeth," he said in an infuriatingly calm voice, "and we were taking our careers in different directions."

"Our personal lives, too."

There was silence. "I look back with fondness on our time together," Jared said at last.

Lizzie wanted to kick him. He sounded so stuffy. They'd been wildly in love. They'd been married for four years. Lizzie had thought Jared was the man she would spend the rest of her life with. Now he acted like she was some kind of brief fling from his faraway youth.

"Can we declare a cessation of hostilities? You're doing me a favor and I know it. I'm in your debt and you know it. How about being a gracious winner?" He held out his hand, and Lizzie slipped hers into it, even though Jared had taken a dig at her.

"Who knows?" he asked as his fingers closed around hers and he gazed into her eyes. "Perhaps one day you'll need me."

Not a chance, was her first thought. *Are you sure?* was her second as the warmth of his fingers triggered equally warm feelings.

She stared at her hand, still grasped by his. Jared had beautiful hands with long, well-shaped fingers. She'd adored watching them as he'd drafted designs, holding the pencil with as much care as he held her.

Slowly, he withdrew his hand. She could feel every ridge of his fingertips as they slid against hers, and she didn't want to let go.

Jared unrolled the plans on her desk. He set her pencil cup on one corner and a glass ashtray filled with candy corn on another.

Back to the present. Lizzie blinked, forcing herself to scan the drawings. "You've got too much wasted space."

"No," Jared disagreed. "I wanted to be certain the wheelchairs could get through."

"Hmm." *Concentrate, Lizzie.* She perched on the edge of her desk and studied Jared's plans, her heart sinking as she realized the amount of alterations the house would require to become competitive with the professional ones. With hers.

"I want this house to raise a hunk of money for the rehab center. They desperately need to expand. If any good can come from my accident, I hope it's making someone else's recovery faster."

Lizzie glanced down at him. "So that's how you hooked up with Hanes Memorial."

Jared grinned. "Yeah. I became tired of waiting for my appointments." His grin faded. "But it was the kids who got to me. I'll heal. Some of them won't."

He stared at the plans, but Lizzie knew he was remembering the children he'd met at the rehab center. She could see the scene as clearly as if he'd described it.

"Oh, Jared," Lizzie moaned and buried her face in her hands. "If there's one thing I can't stand, it's disappointing children. But my houses take weeks to build. You don't have time this year." She lowered her hands and looked at him. "And as it is, yours won't... I'm sorry. Really."

His chin jutted, ever so slightly. "Then modify the existing structure."

Lizzie shook her head. "I'm swamped. Completely booked. Even modifying this design would require a lot of time. I—"

Jared took both her hands in his. "Please?"

The rat. Gazing up at her from a wheelchair. Pleading for injured children. How could she refuse without feeling like an ogre?

She couldn't.

Sighing, she warned, "It'll be tight. And expensive."

Jared smiled in satisfaction. "I knew you'd come through."

Lizzie already regretted her capitulation. "I'm not kidding about the money. You'll have to budget for overtime and rush delivery. It might not be cost-effective."

"Don't worry about the money." Jared dismissed it as a minor problem. "My parents are having a little fund-raiser tonight at their home. That's one reason I'm in Houston."

"They arranged it before you knew I'd agree to help you?" And she'd thought he was in Houston just to see her.

Jared rolled backward. "They know no one can withstand their son's charming personality."

Lizzie searched for something to throw.

"I'll pick you up at seven-thirty. Black tie." He wheeled around and headed for the door.

"I'm not going!"

"But you have to come."

"I wasn't invited." Jared's parents would never willingly invite her to anything.

"Consider yourself invited," Jared said negligently. "Who better to convince these people to invest heavily in your haunted house?"

"Did it occur to you that I might have other plans?" Lizzie followed him to the hall.

"Nope." He grinned over his shoulder. "Carleen said you were free."

"Carleen doesn't book my personal time!" Lizzie said loudly, for Carleen's benefit. "And speaking of plans, when do you expect me to draw them?"

"You've got all day. You only need a few sketches. These people aren't architects."

"A few sketches!" Lizzie began to burn. "My houses need a lot more than a few sketches!"

"Whatever. Just finish by seven-thirty." He rolled out of sight.

"Jared!"

He rolled back, wearing a smug expression.

"*If* I go," she stressed, "I'll meet you there. It's too much trouble for you to pick me up."

"I insist. But you might wait outside. That walkway is murder. Oh, one other thing." He looked her up and down. "These are conservative folks."

Lizzie raised an eyebrow. "What are you implying?"

He nodded to her blinking skull pin. "Leave the flashing jewelry at home."

"I *like* flashing jewelry." Lizzie crossed her arms.

"Elizabeth," Jared said sternly. "Try not to embarrass me."

Slowly, regally, Lizzie squeezed past Jared and glided to the front door, holding it open for him. A thick plywood plank, bolstered by Carleen and Edward, now lay over the steps. "I wouldn't dream of it, Jared."

Jared paused in the doorway and studied her face.

Lizzie smiled.

With a final warning look, Jared rolled down the plank.

IF ONLY SHE HAD THE NERVE to prance out to meet him wearing a black tie and nothing else.

It took nearly as much nerve to wear the dress she had on now. She'd ordered it out of a catalog, and when it had arrived, it turned out to be one of those dresses that she wanted to lose five pounds before wearing.

Of course, she'd never lost the five pounds and she'd never worn the dress before, either. Orange paillettes glittered on a flesh-colored silk slip dress that hugged every curve. It ended at mid-thigh.

To complete the outfit, Lizzie had misted her hair until every curl kinked wildly. Crystal pumpkins twinkled at her ears. Gray eyeshadow smoked her eyes. Orange-sequined sneakers gleamed on her feet.

Jared would be shocked.

Jared would disapprove.

Lizzie could hardly wait.

AT PRECISELY seven twenty-seven, Jared pulled his specially equipped van into Elizabeth's driveway. He'd allowed extra time in case she wasn't waiting for him.

But she was. And she was wearing the most outrageous piece of clothing she possessed. He knew that without even looking at her.

What better way to ensure her presence at the fundraiser than asking her not to embarrass him? She'd come just to do that.

Jared smiled to himself when he remembered the expression on her face when he'd left this morning. He was in for a very difficult time tonight, but all for a good cause. If he'd finessed his way around Elizabeth years ago instead of meeting her head-on, they might still be married.

He shuddered. Scary thought.

On the drive over, he'd amused himself by trying to imagine her costume for the evening. Discarding the intriguing possibility that she might wear nothing but a black tie, he decided she'd probably shroud herself in black, wear white makeup and carry a broom.

Elizabeth moved out of the shadows. Jared caught his breath as she minced over the flagstones, stopped at the passenger side of his van and tossed in a cardboard tube. That little orange number was no shroud.

She eyed the step up. Jared eyed her hemline.

Then he eyed her neckline—if Elizabeth weren't careful, the two would meet.

She looked at him through her lashes, then hitched what there was of her dress higher, gave a tiny wiggly hop and swung her legs into the van.

"Nicely done." Jared applauded.

Elizabeth ignored him, tugged her skirt down a fraction of an inch and fastened her seatbelt. She stared straight ahead.

Jared stared at her. Elizabeth had always done the unexpected. He'd once been charmed by her audacity, until it had become commonplace.

And now? Now he was merely amused.

Elizabeth's head jerked around, sending her earrings swinging. Sparkly balls on long chains brushed her bare shoulders. Jared peered close. Pumpkins. Elizabeth was wearing pumpkin earrings.

"What are you staring at?" she snapped.

"You."

"Why?"

Jared grinned. "Don't you want people to stare at you?"

Her chin tilted upward. Obviously she thought he was going to criticize her dress. Not a chance. That was one trap he'd avoid.

"Well-bred people do not stare. I understood that this was to be a gathering of well-bred people."

"Most of them," Jared murmured as he started the van and backed out of the drive.

"How did you do that?" Elizabeth asked, with alarm.

"Hand controls. Has it only now occurred to you to wonder how I've been driving this thing?"

"I assumed that since your legs aren't paralyzed, you just..." Elizabeth trailed off as she examined the controls.

"I could, but the van came equipped like this. I rented it from the clinic."

"Pretty nifty."

"Pretty nifty," Jared agreed.

Elizabeth seemed nervous, he noted. She continually glanced at his hands, watching him as he drove. "Relax," he said. "I've had a lot of practice. I drove all the way from Dallas. It was easier than dealing with the airport."

"You drove here by yourself?"

"No. I brought someone with me."

"Anyone I know?"

Jared hesitated. "Helen Travis."

The atmosphere inside the van turned chilly.

"I might have known she'd still be hanging around."

"Elizabeth," Jared said on a sigh. "Don't start."

"Our truce did *not* include that stuck-up dishwater blonde," Elizabeth snapped.

"I hope you'll feel differently when you see her again."

"I doubt it."

She was in one of those moods. Now was not the time to tell her.... Jared remained silent out of long practice. The evening ahead was going to be worse than he thought.

He merged onto the Sam Houston Tollway and eventually Elizabeth unwound, chatting about inconsequentials until he parked the van in front of his parents' house. Then she visibly stiffened.

"My parents are looking forward to seeing you again," he reassured her as they entered the gracious home.

"Yeah, right. Tell me another story." She threw him a disgusted glance.

Okay, maybe "looking forward" was a bit strong. "Warily tolerant" might better describe his parents' state of mind concerning Elizabeth.

Many of the guests had already arrived. Somehow, his parents had managed to assemble an impressive number of people on short notice. He wished for equally impressive donations.

He glanced up at Elizabeth. Would she behave herself this evening? Surely wearing that dress in this company would be enough rebellion for anyone. She was right about one thing. This was a well-bred crowd, and the people would be too polite to remark on her dress—or her shoes.

It was then that he noticed the black shoelaces. Black ties. He reached for her hand to tell her he appreciated the joke, but she had walked on ahead.

He remained near the foyer, unwilling to negotiate a path through the crowd, and entertained himself by observing her.

She saw him watching her and tossed the unruly mane of her hair, grabbed a glass of champagne and began to mingle. Jared chuckled and shook his head, refusing to let her annoy him.

"Darling! There you are." A tall, wintry blonde appeared at his side.

Jared smiled. "You're lovely as always. Helen."

She looked at the white pleated gown she wore, touching the gold trim at the neck. "You don't think my dress is too plain?" Helen glanced over her shoulder, and Jared knew she was thinking of Elizabeth.

"It's perfect," he said with heartfelt sincerity. Helen was very restful. He didn't need to be on guard for what she'd do next.

Helen smiled at him and leaned down to whisper. "Is she behaving herself?"

"So far." Jared followed Elizabeth's progress across the room. She was putting on quite a show for his benefit.

"I see she's just as irreverent as ever," Helen noted. "I hope no one is offended."

Offend was a rather strong word. "Helen, we do require her help. Please don't antagonize her."

"I wouldn't dream of it." She squeezed his shoulder. "We only have to put up with her for a few weeks."

A few excruciating weeks, he thought. Elizabeth caught his eye, glanced at Helen and smirked. Jared's father tapped his former daughter-in-law on the shoulder and spoke to her briefly. Elizabeth nodded, then began walking toward them.

As she approached, Jared made the inevitable comparison between the two women. Helen was tall and slim and regal.

Elizabeth was fire and light and movement.

"Your parents want everyone to see the drawings now, Jared," she said, then turned to Helen. "Hello, Helen. How's tricks?"

I should have told her. Conscious that he'd made a tactical error, Jared braced himself as Helen slid a possessive arm around his shoulders. "Jared and I are so glad you're able to help us, Elizabeth. Now that we're beyond all the unpleasantness, perhaps you'll be able to come to the wedding."

"Wedding?" Elizabeth quirked an eyebrow at Jared.

Jared's collar suddenly tightened. He cleared his throat and attempted a hearty smile. "Helen is my fiancée."

CHAPTER FOUR

FIANCÉE. The lights went dim.

Lizzie swallowed. The party chatter sounded very far away.

Triumph glittered in Helen's eyes. *Helen.* Why hadn't Jared told her? Then again, why should he?

Because. Because it was Helen. Helen Travis, the bane of Lizzie's existence. The favorite of Jared's mother. Helen, the perfect. Helen, who always seemed to be available for family gatherings during the holidays.

Helen, who never put on a single *pound* during those holidays.

Helen was tall. Lizzie was medium. Helen was the graduate of an expensive finishing school. Lizzie was unfinished. Helen, the pianist, had traveled all over the world. Lizzie had taken three clarinet lessons in the seventh grade and hadn't been anywhere more exotic than Girl Scout camp.

Elegant Helen.

Frizzy Lizzie.

Maybe Jared didn't think she cared whether he married again. And she shouldn't. So why did she?

The happy couple was waiting for her reaction. Lizzie held out her hand. "Congratulations," she offered pleasantly. The instant the word was out of her mouth, Lizzie remembered that one congratulated the groom and offered best wishes to the bride. She was sure Helen would notice.

Helen grasped her hand briefly. "Thank you. This must be a trifle awkward for you."

Lizzie bared her teeth. "Not at all." She sent a you-could-have-warned-me glare to Jared.

He regarded her silently, his dark eyes unreadable. "Time to present the drawings." He maneuvered his wheelchair between the two women. "This project means a lot to me," he reminded them, then rolled into the well-bred throng.

As she walked beside Helen, Lizzie regretted not wearing her one and only pair of pumps, in spite of the fact that the orange sequins on her tennis shoes exactly matched her dress. She wanted the height. She wanted to tower over Helen, instead of being towered over. She wanted to intimidate, but when had she ever intimidated anyone?

Lizzie checked out Helen's hand to see if the engagement ring had a diamond bigger than the one Jared had given her. No ring. Hmm. And she'd thought diamonds were a ghoul's best friend.

Lizzie's eyes sought Jared's. He waited beside a flip chart set up next to the fireplace, a watchful expression on his face.

Did he really think she was unprofessional enough to have a catfight with Helen? As if she'd dream of doing such a thing.

Here.

Not ever confronting Helen was Lizzie's only regret. During her marriage to Jared, she'd endured countless barbs from Helen and her mother as well as Jared's mother. Genteel barbs that made Lizzie appear petty if she reacted. An oblivious Jared couldn't understand why Lizzie and Helen didn't get along.

The day she'd moved out, Lizzie had discovered she'd left her favorite mechanical pencil in the desk drawer. Since she'd only driven a few blocks, she'd turned around and gone back to the house.

When she'd arrived, Helen's car was pulling into the driveway. As she'd watched Helen emerge in all her white pantsuited glory, Lizzie had forced herself to continue on instead of leaping out and engaging in a little shoving and hair pulling. The thought of grass stains on Helen's outfit had been tempting; the thought of Jared's disgust had been depressing.

Jared was speaking. "Welcome and thank you for coming. We're here tonight..."

Her attention wandered as Jared explained his project. Helen listened serenely, publicly standing by her man.

And Lizzie had to admit, Jared was some man. She tried to study him objectively and unemotionally and found she couldn't. What was it about him that still had the power to affect her?

He was attractive, certainly, but so were other men, and she felt nothing for them. His suit was dark and expensive, the pants slit at the seam to accommodate the cast on his foot. He looked at ease, even though he was confined to the wheelchair.

As Lizzie's gaze roved around the room, she encountered Jared's parents, who acknowledged her with polite, if frosty, nods.

Jared's parents had never approved of her. Lizzie's solidly middle-class background wasn't upwardly mobile enough for their precious Jared. But Helen... Helen was the daughter-in-law of their dreams. Someone worthy of being Mrs. Jared Rutledge. Someone worthy of bearing the Rutledge heirs.

Lizzie straightened her shoulders and stole another peek at Helen's classically perfect profile before returning her attention to Jared.

Just in time. "Elizabeth Wilcox, who is a nationally known designer of entertainment works of this kind," how impressive she sounded, "has agreed to act as consultant on this project. She's already suggested several changes that will improve the basic design. I'll let her tell you about them."

Jared smiled at her, and Lizzie, conscious of all the eyes on her and her dress, joined him at the flip chart.

The sketches she'd drawn were rough, just hinting at what could be built, but Lizzie was a veteran of countless similar presentations. During this one, she stressed the short time frame and resulting cost increases, but balanced the information with the enhanced revenues the clinic could expect.

Jared listened attentively. Lizzie could tell he was surprised at her persuasive speech. He shouldn't be; she'd given dozens of these speeches.

"It's a gamble," Lizzie concluded. "You have a nearly complete house now. It won't be a big moneymaker, but you'll draw some traffic. But with my modifications and marketing, you'll triple, at least, your gate receipts."

"Maybe not triple," Jared said, but he was drowned out by the murmurs of approval.

"I think you can, Jared." Lizzie raised her voice. "My reputation will attract people." She spoke with the confidence of one who knew she was needed.

"Elizabeth." Jared smiled, but his eyes flashed a warning, "We mustn't mislead these good people."

"I'm sure these *good people* appreciate your caution on their behalf, Jared," Lizzie said. "But if I lend my name to this project, it's going to be a pull-out-all-the-stops effort. You have three weeks. This is no time to be timid." And it was no time for Jared to disagree with her. How dare he challenge her opinions during her presentation? They should appear united.

"If the clinic is so desperate for funds and equipment, why not give the money directly to them rather than risking it on a haunted house?" asked a businessman.

Jared cleared his throat, obviously preparing to respond to him.

"We're proposing to build a semipermanent structure," Lizzie answered before Jared could collect his thoughts. Why didn't he trust her to do her job? She'd heard this question once during every presentation she'd ever made. "The initial costs should be recouped the first year and subsequent yearly operations will provide income for the clinic." She paused, allowing the potential donors to assimilate the information. "Your gifts will keep on giving." Okay, so it wasn't original. It was still effective.

"But...but the medical center grounds are so pretty," protested a brocaded matron. "And this..." she trailed off with a gesture.

"In other cities, we've invited local artists to paint murals on the outside of the building. It provides them with exposure and camouflages the house. Then, once a year, the building is repainted and other artists have their chance."

As the people began to talk among themselves, Lizzie glanced at Jared. He looked stunned. That'll teach him to underestimate *her,* she thought with well-deserved satisfaction.

"If haunted houses are such money-makers, why not operate it all year?" Businessman number one again.

"You could, but experience has shown me that it wouldn't be cost-effective. And you might burn out your volunteers. A six-week operation is the most I recommend. A month is better."

Lizzie answered questions for a minute more. To her surprise, Helen was the first to applaud when she finished.

"It's such a shame we can't see one of your houses, Elizabeth," she said.

"You can. I designed the Dungeon of Doom at Buffalo Bayou Mall. It's complete, though it doesn't open until next weekend." Lizzie hesitated, then offered, "Mall management has agreed to let us tour it, if you like." She was amused at the thought of this stuffy crowd promenading through a haunted house in their evening clothes.

"That's a wonderful idea!" Helen turned to Jared's parents, who had joined them. "Don't you think?"

"I do," Jared agreed. "Did you mean right now, Elizabeth?"

Lizzie was nodding when Jared's mother interrupted. "Oh, but we'd hoped Helen would play for us." She waved imperiously toward the piano. "Just dash off a quick something, dear."

Lizzie felt that familiar sinking sensation she'd experienced when faced with Helen's tremendous talent. She stifled a groan, before noticing Helen's expression. For a brief moment, Lizzie thought she saw a flash of resentment, then Helen was walking toward the gleaming ebony grand piano tucked in the curve of the staircase.

A hush fell over the room. Obviously, this crowd had heard Helen play before. Lizzie was glad. She became very annoyed when people talked during one of Helen's performances. Helen wasn't her favorite person in the world, but Lizzie acknowledged her mastery of the piano.

She sensed Jared next to her, then was caught up in the music. Helen tossed off glittering runs and powerful chords as the melody grew in intensity before crashing to a close.

In the seconds before the applause began, Helen's eyes met hers. Lizzie managed a tremulous smile, aware that her cheeks were wet.

A white linen handkerchief appeared in her line of vision. "Thanks," she mumbled to Jared.

"Helen's playing always did affect you that way," he commented as Lizzie blotted her cheeks.

"I'm just an emotional person, I guess." No one else was blubbering. Why couldn't she remain blasé like the other women?

"I've always thought that was part of your charm," he said quietly.

Lizzie looked at him in surprise. "And I thought it got on your nerves."

A corner of his mouth tilted upward. "A little does go a long way."

As Lizzie chuckled, their gazes caught and held. Her smile faded. The old awareness stretched between them until it was broken by Jared's mother.

"That was very nice, Helen."

Lizzie blinked, surprised to find that Helen had rejoined them.

"You never learned to play, did you, Elizabeth?" asked Mrs. Rutledge.

Lizzie shook her head. Jared's mother always expressed disappointment that Lizzie couldn't perform.

"We all have our different strengths, Mother." There was the merest hint of admonition in Jared's voice.

"And Elizabeth is going to make the clinic piles of money," Helen said, to Lizzie's utter astonishment. Support from Helen? Against Jared's mother? This was a first.

"Quite." Mrs. Rutledge attempted a social smile, but her heart obviously wasn't in it. "So, Elizabeth, when may we tour one of your structures?"

Lizzie rallied. "Now, if you like."

"I'm not certain that now is—"

"Come on, Mother," Jared urged. "Just think of how it will read in the society columns."

He continued to point out the intriguing publicity angles and soon his mother was organizing a caravan to Buffalo Bayou Mall.

An hour later, Lizzie faced the group of potential donors at the entrance to the Dungeon of Doom. In a way, this would actually be her performance. "And this year, you'll only be able to open on Halloween, so you want to admit as many people as you can."

She unlocked the door. "This design is normally operated by nine actors. There's no guide because that takes too much time. I'll leave the lights on and explain what happens in each area."

She tapped the wall opposite the entry. "This is a false panel, concealing an actor. Immediately after and sometimes during the group's entrance, they're startled. The crowd waiting hears their screams and it heightens the anticipation. It also serves to move each group into the house so you can admit the next bunch."

Lizzie urged her group around a black corner. "You want people to be startled from all directions except the front. They should never be afraid to proceed into your house."

"I thought the idea was to just frighten them," Jared said.

"The group should be afraid to stay in one place," Lizzie replied. "That's why you sometimes let the first few pass, then scare the stragglers forward. Always remember, scare forward."

"What if they miss something?" he asked.

"Make them pay to see it again," Lizzie answered promptly. "Repeat business." She could tell that this concept found favor with the men in the group. The women looked uncertain. "Don't worry," Lizzie assured them, "everyone will get his money's worth."

She continued, explaining how patterns of light kept people moving and demonstrating how sensors triggered roars and screams. She was conscious of Jared and his wheelchair the entire time. He negotiated all but the sloping floors easily. Lizzie made a mental note to keep floors level in Jared's house.

As the group exited, Jared wheeled over to her. "Haunted houses have certainly changed since we built our first one."

Lizzie nodded, waiting for his reaction and loathing the fact that she cared about it at all.

"It all seems so calculated." He didn't sound as though that pleased him, which irritated Lizzie.

"It's a business. My business."

He gazed at her briefly before conceding her point with an abrupt nod. "I realize how tame the house I designed is in comparison. I'd like to see this one operating, though. I'm concerned about the number of laborers we'll need. Who has time to train them?"

"It's not hard." Lizzie was willing to be generous.

Jared shook his head. "Maybe not for you."

Lizzie grinned. "Not for anybody. Watch."

She strode toward the center of the knot of people and clapped her hands for attention. "I need nine folks who'd like to scare the rest of you as you tour the house again."

When she had her nine volunteers, Lizzie took them inside the house and positioned them. She showed them how to operate various "startles" and then turned off the lights.

"Ready?" she called out the door.

Lizzie pretended to take tickets and admitted the Rutledges' guests. Squeals, laughter and screams, both human and inhuman, reverberated through the house.

"Now it's our turn," Jared informed her. "I want to see if I can negotiate the house in the dark."

Lizzie hesitated, then followed him inside.

"Boo!" yelled the first monster, behind a false wall. It turned out to be Jared's mother, giggling and having the time of her life.

Sequined bodies lurked in boo corners and men in expensive suits squatted in backstage areas operating noisemakers and eerie lights.

Lizzie and Jared ran into the group bunched at the outside of a crypt. She squeezed in front of him to see what had held everyone up. "There should be a green light coming on," she called. "This is a good example of the way you can regulate how fast the groups travel through your house."

"Oooooh," moaned a plump monster in chiffon, who then stumbled against Lizzie. Lizzie backed up and tripped over Jared, falling into his lap.

Jared, no doubt reacting instinctively, grabbed her.

Lizzie clutched first at her hemline, then at her composure, as she found herself held securely against Jared's chest.

"Oops!" The chiffon monster regained her balance before laughing and disappearing behind a door.

The rest of the group moved on.

Lizzie tried not to move at all.

Back in Jared's arms after three years. Three impossibly long years. She'd never wanted the divorce, never believed it would really happen until she held the papers in her hands.

They were two pigheaded people who should have tried harder to iron out their differences.

And now it was too late. Even though Lizzie wanted nothing more than to mold herself to Jared and put her arms around his neck, she wouldn't.

Her legs ached with the effort of holding her body stiff. How was she going to extricate herself? She tried relaxing one leg, searching for the floor in the blackness.

"You still wear the same perfume," Jared murmured and inhaled deeply. "It always smells warm."

Lizzie froze as tingles skipped down her spine.

This would never do. Jared had chosen another woman. He was unavailable. She should do her best to remain tingleproof.

Lizzie shifted her body experimentally. Jared's arms tightened around her.

A rich chuckle told her he was enjoying her discomfort. "Jared," she scolded. "Let me up."

"Why? You used to like being held by me."

"Have you forgotten Helen?"

"Of course not." Jared released her immediately, and Lizzie struggled to her feet.

Their breathing sounded loud in the inky darkness.

"We'd better rejoin the others," Jared said finally.

Lizzie walked behind his chair and pushed.

"I've got it," Jared said, and Lizzie stepped back. Way back.

The rest of their tour proceeded smoothly. When they emerged from the house, the guests were clustered together, talking animatedly.

"Elizabeth," Jared's father addressed her. "How much will it cost to redesign the Dallas house?"

She gave him a figure. His eyes widened. He stared at her as he mentally calculated, then returned to the group. Within minutes, Jared had collected checks totaling several thousand dollars.

He and Helen graciously thanked each of the donors. Lizzie stood to one side, trying not to feel like the hired help.

Didn't anyone realize she'd come to Jared's rescue?

Apparently Jared did. "Letting those people run the Dungeon of Doom was brilliant," he said later as he drove Lizzie home. Helen had accompanied Jared's parents. "I can't believe that we raised all the money right then. Right then," he repeated. "You're amazing."

Lizzie basked in Jared's praise. His words reminded her of another time and another place. Back when they'd collaborated on their first haunted house and Jared had been constantly amazed by the number of ideas she'd had. That was the way they functioned.

Lizzie had the ideas, and Jared translated them onto paper.

However, this was no time for nostalgia, sentiment or what-might-have-beens.

"Thanks. But I've had plenty of practice raising funds for my haunted houses."

"Still, I'm impressed," Jared insisted, doing nothing for Lizzie's peace of mind. "My parents' friends are a conservative bunch."

Lizzie remembered him telling her that earlier. "They had a good time tonight. Now they understand what's involved in running a haunted house," she said, adding, "All we have to do is build it."

"ELIZABETH WILCOX! Are you asleep on that sofa again?"

Lizzie opened her eyes, immediately shutting them against the bright sunlight that burned through the floor-to-ceiling windows in her living room.

Drat. She hadn't spent a night in her bed since Jared's parents' little soiree.

"I'm awake," she croaked.

Obviously she didn't fool Carleen. "No, you're not. Make yourself decent, I'm coming in."

Lizzie pulled a pillow over her face and regretted giving Carleen a key to her apartment.

The door swung open. "Decent as usual," Carleen said in disgust. "If you consider that getup decent."

"Wharongwifit?"

"A giant T-shirt, mismatched knee socks, bunny slippers and your father's old bathrobe—everything's wrong with it. Do you even own anything decent to be indecent in?"

"Mmph."

"I didn't think so." A small thud sounded next to Lizzie's ear.

She pulled the pillow down from her face, ready to inform Carleen that her sleeping attire and sleeping location were none of Carleen's business when she saw the cup of coffee in her line of vision. "Thanks," she said instead and slowly sat up.

"No problem." Carleen had already moved into the kitchen where she would encounter the remains of a frozen dinner cementing a fork to a microwave disposable plate.

"Just leave that. I'll get to it," Lizzie called and sipped her coffee.

Running water told her that Carleen had ignored her as usual. Lizzie was too exhausted to press the point.

Moments later, Carleen strode back into the living room and stopped in front of the sofa, hands on hips. "What kept you up this time?"

Lizzie stared into her coffee cup.

Carleen bent down and poked through the sketches on the low table next to the sofa. "A brand-new design?"

Lizzie nodded.

"For *this* Halloween?"

Sheepishly, Lizzie nodded again.

"Elizabeth Wilcox, has someone blown out the light in your pumpkin? What possessed you to take on another job?"

Lizzie sighed. "It's for Jared."

Carleen crossed her arms. "I thought you were only consulting."

"I am."

"This—" Carleen gathered up Lizzie's drawings "—is a lot more than consulting."

"Call it a favor for old times' sake." Lizzie stood and stretched. Her neck and shoulder burned, and she massaged the tender areas.

"Were the old times that good?"

"Carleen . . ."

"Besides, I thought he'd already built a house."

"A grossly inadequate house."

"I should never have let you talk to him." Carleen straightened the rest of the papers on the coffee table and moved to Lizzie's drafting board. She returned pencils to their holder and swept eraser shavings into the wastebasket.

"Hey, you hounded me into talking to him!" Lizzie's mind was beginning to function again.

"A decision that shall come back to haunt me." Carleen stooped and picked up the pair of green tennis shoes with orange chiffon laces Lizzie had worn yesterday. She gazed around the room, spied two pairs of discarded earrings and Lizzie's jacket, added those to her armful and headed toward Lizzie's bedroom.

"Carleen, you don't have to straighten up." Lizzie shuffled after her and plopped down on the bed.

"I raised five kids. I'm used to it." Carleen stood in front of Lizzie's closet. "What are you wearing today?"

"I don't know."

"Hmm." Carleen flipped through Lizzie's clothes. "You have a site inspection in Austin."

Lizzie groaned and muttered under her breath.

"No, I won't reschedule. You'll only regret it later," Carleen said sternly and pulled out a brown, cream and black leopard print blouse with a coordinating jacket and city shorts. She tossed the outfit at Lizzie and found matching leopard print tennis shoes.

"I didn't ask you to reschedule."

"You were about to."

"What if I was?"

Carleen sat on the edge of the bed, shaking her head. "You're killing yourself, and I'm not going to let you."

Lizzie tried to shrug off Carleen's concern. "I hired you to be my secretary slash receptionist slash bookkeeper. There's no slash mother in your job description."

"I'd hoped I was also a slash friend." Hurt tinged Carleen's voice.

"You are," Lizzie reassured her quickly.

"Besides, if you croak, I'll be out of a job."

"Carleen!"

"So what are you trying to prove by staying up all night three nights in a row?"

"Nothing," Lizzie frowned and drained her coffee.

"Yes, you are. You're still in love with Jared and you hope that by creating a spectacular house for him, you'll show him how blind he's been all these years. He'll be so dazzled, he'll fall to his knees and beg you to take him back, right?"

Close enough to make Lizzie uncomfortable. Close enough to force her to level with Carleen. "With one exception. Helen Travis, his fiancée."

"Oh."

With a shrug of her shoulders meant to show that she didn't care, Lizzie moved over to her vanity and tried to untangle her curls.

"So how are you going to break them up?"

"I'm not."

"You mean you aren't going to fight for your man?"

Lizzie dragged a brush through her hair so hard tears pooled in her eyes. "Jared isn't my man. He hasn't been for years. In fact, two weeks ago I wouldn't have imagined that we'd be discussing him like this."

"Then why bother designing a new house for him? You don't have time."

"Call it a wedding present."

"I will not."

Lizzie smiled.

"Tell me about her," Carleen urged. "What are her weaknesses?"

"She doesn't have any." Very gently, Lizzie set the brush on her bureau. "She's perfect for him. Think of my exact opposite. Tall, blonde and elegant, with a touch of cool reserve."

"Maybe she's too tall?" a loyal Carleen suggested.

Lizzie shook her head. "She's perfect."

"Too perfect?"

Lizzie opened her mouth to deny it, then stopped. That was it. Too perfect.

Helen would rarely disagree and never throw a tantrum. She'd make a perfect wife, all right.

For someone else.

CHAPTER FIVE

TWO DAYS LATER, Lizzie flew to Dallas, new plans for the Hanes Memorial Haunted House rolled in a tube that was tucked under her arm. She'd spent hours on the changes. It would've been easier to start fresh, but she wanted to use as much of Jared's design as possible. She hoped he appreciated her gesture.

"Where have you been?" Jared, now on crutches, met her at the site.

"Greetings to you, too." So much for his appreciation.

"I was beginning to worry. I've been waiting for more than an hour." Jared began picking a path through the clumps of dirt and building debris.

"I have other projects besides this one," Lizzie reminded him. She tilted her head to one side, watching him. It was the first time she'd seen him upright since his accident. Even hunched over the crutches, he still loomed above her. "Were you really worried about me?"

"Of course!" He appeared surprised that she'd ask. "We can't get started without your plans."

The plans. Of course. Lizzie sighed. "I had material orders faxed to you."

"Yes, I know." Jared thumped his way toward the house. "Who's Edward?"

"My assistant."

"I'd prefer to deal with you."

Lizzie snorted. "That's a switch."

Jared stopped and chuckled. "Yeah. It's a crazy idea when you think about it—the two of us, associated with the same project at the same time?" He shook his head and swung his injured foot over the threshold. "Time to lower the dose on my pain medication."

Lizzie drew a deep breath between her teeth, kicked dirt off her hot pink tennis shoes and followed Jared inside.

He waited by the crypt. Wordlessly, she unrolled her plans.

Jared scanned them and whistled. "No wonder you ordered so much lumber." He studied the plans a few seconds more, then turned to her. "Elizabeth, couldn't you have designed something simpler?"

He was supposed to be astounded at her intricate design. He was supposed to compliment her. "You have something simpler already."

"I know, but—" he gestured to the plans "—I don't think we can build this in three weeks."

"Sure you can. Though if there's any sort of delay, you won't finish in time," she warned. "Just bribe the carpenters. They love overtime."

"We're using volunteer help. Didn't I mention that?" he asked casually.

What? "No, you did not!" Lizzie muttered a very unHelenlike word under her breath.

Volunteer labor . . . was he mad? Maybe to paint and run the thing, but on the actual construction of the house? Once more, Jared had unintentionally demonstrated exactly what he thought of her business. "How could you even *consider* using unskilled labor to build one of my houses?"

"That's how we built this one," Jared said in surprise. "It's just a haunted house, not the Taj Mahal."

Lizzie flung her arms out. "Compared to this house, mine *is* the Taj Mahal!"

"And it'll probably cost as much to build!"

They glared at each other.

Lizzie had only wanted him to acknowledge the difficulties of her designs. If he couldn't acknowledge her desirability as a woman, she wanted his recognition of her as a peer. "I wouldn't have designed such a complicated haunted house if I'd known you were using volunteers. I'll redraw the plans." She heard the wobble in her voice and cleared her throat. "But I honestly don't know when."

"Shh!" Jared stared off in the distance, thinking. Lizzie shushed.

She'd promised herself that the Haunted Hotel would be her first priority. She'd carefully scheduled her time. She'd delegated to Edward. She'd humored Carleen.

Jared was wrecking everything.

Perhaps the design *was* too complicated. What had possessed her? In trying to impress him, she'd gone overboard. "I might as well get started on the modifications." She reached for her drawings.

Jared leaned against the crypt, freeing one hand. He grabbed her wrist. "Leave them."

"No," Lizzie said, conscious of his touch. "There's no way you can build a house like this in three weeks—"

"Could you?" he challenged.

"Sure."

"Then I can, if you can."

"Don't be silly." Lizzie jerked her arm away, reflexively rubbing the spot where Jared had held it. "I build this kind of house all the time."

"I always knew you were nuts."

"That's it!" Lizzie pirouetted, ready to march right out of there.

Jared guessed her intention and grabbed her arm again. "And I mean that in the nicest possible way." He accompanied this with the widest fake smile Lizzie had ever seen.

"Forgot how much you needed my help, right?" She smiled. Sweetly.

Jared nodded. "Not an intelligent move on my part. I offer you my humblest and most profound apology."

Lizzie scowled at him, at his hand on her arm and back at him. He was in a spot and knew it. "You're really desperate, aren't you?" she asked. "Really, *really* desperate."

"Yes," he admitted. "What will your staying cost me?"

Lizzie considered. "Groveling. Serious groveling."

Jared released her. "With or without bribes?"

"Oh, with. Definitely with."

"Animal, mineral or vegetable?"

"Is chocolate a vegetable?"

A corner of his mouth quirked. "How about a refill for your M&M's dispenser?"

"Jared, Jared, Jared." Lizzie shook her head. "Nowadays, I find an assortment of Godiva truffles helps me concentrate."

Jared raised her eyebrows. "I'll bet."

"I'll share," she offered with an impish grin.

"I see the price of groveling has gone up like everything else." He regarded her for a moment. "Okay."

"Great. Give me a day or two," Lizzie said, reaching for the drawings again, "and I'll have another set ready."

"No." Jared scrutinized the curling blueprints. "This is possible," he murmured, as if thinking aloud. "I'll oversee the project. I'll hammer right along with the volunteers. I'll even hire carpenters."

"And *I'll* revise—free of charge." Lizzie was feeling generous.

"I said *no.*"

Jared's voice was so unexpectedly harsh that Lizzie flinched.

"I wanted a Wilcox house, and I've got a Wilcox house. You just told me you build houses like this all the time. Anything less is unacceptable."

Oh, no. He was looking at this as a test of his abilities. That hadn't been Lizzie's intention at all. She'd wanted him to be impressed with *her* abilities. What a mess.

"You can have a simpler Wilcox house. My mistake." If she stressed that, then he could salvage his pride.

"Don't you touch that design!" He grabbed the plans.

"It's my design, and I'll touch it if I want to!" Lizzie snatched them back.

"Give me those plans!"

"No!"

Lizzie and Jared glared at each other.

"Settled down, children." Helen, picnic hamper in hand, peered at them with distaste.

"Helen!" Jared greeted her with a little too much cheer, in Lizzie's opinion.

Helen presented her cheek, and he dutifully kissed it. Lizzie used the opportunity to roll up the plans in anticipation of a quick getaway.

"It sounds as if you need a break." Helen opened the hamper and pulled out a cloth, which she draped over the coffin.

"I think that's an excellent suggestion," Lizzie said. Good grief, she was beginning to sound like Jared's mother. "I'll leave you two to your lunch and get a—"

"Elizabeth, I brought enough for you as well. Please stay." Helen handed her a sandwich.

"Thanks." Lizzie perched on the tomb supporting the coffin and crossed her legs. Jared half leaned, half sat on the edge. With a grimace at the coffin, Helen sank to the floor.

"Now, what was the argument about?" She handed a canned soft drink to Jared and a diet one to Lizzie. Lizzie decided nothing was meant by it.

In fact, she thought, biting into the sandwich, Helen might help her convince Jared to let her do another, less intricate design.

"We were just squabbling, Helen," Jared said.

Squabbling? What kind of a word was that? Lizzie almost gagged on her egg salad sandwich. "Jared is being gallant. My design is too complex for the amount of time he has to build the house. I want to simplify the design." Lizzie thought she sounded sweetly reasonable.

Apparently Helen thought so, too. "What's wrong with that, Jared?"

Jared sent Lizzie a dark look.

Lizzie batted her eyelashes.

"I wanted a Wilcox house. Elizabeth has designed one. End of discussion."

"Well, there you are, Elizabeth," Helen pronounced. "The plans remain as is. You do remember how determined Jared can be when he decides something. Don't you?" She softened her words with a fond glance at him.

Lizzie lost her appetite. She'd never really liked egg salad, anyway.

On the other hand, Helen had extended the sandwich of friendship. Lizzie needed to reciprocate. "I enjoyed your playing the other night." It was a compliment she sincerely meant. "What was that piece?"

"Chopin. 'The Ballade in G-minor.'" Helen smiled a strange smile. "You're the only one who asked."

As soon as they'd eaten, Jared hopped upright on his good foot and grabbed his crutches. "I've got to call the local union for some carpenters, if we hope to have even a prayer of opening this Halloween."

"You're the one who insisted that I not simplify the design," Lizzie grumbled.

"And don't you touch it while I'm gone. Helen, guard those plans."

If Helen hadn't been there, Lizzie would have stuck her tongue out at him.

As Jared hobbled through the doorway, Helen turned to Lizzie. "I'm glad we have this chance to chat."

Lizzie hoped Helen wasn't planning to launch into one of those let's-be-friends-for-Jared's-sake chats. She and Helen would never be friends. They could, however, be civil to each other for the next three weeks. Then Lizzie would never have to see either Helen—or Jared—again.

She practiced a civil smile.

There was no answering civility from Helen. "I appreciate your helping us with this project and understand that you'll be working closely with Jared. However, I will not tolerate any of your pathetic attempts to get him back."

Lizzie's eyes widened.

"Oh, don't look at me like that," Helen continued. "You hate the fact that I'm going to marry Jared, and you'd do anything to break us up."

Lizzie hadn't thought anything of the sort. "Like *you* wanted to break *us* up?" It was a shot in the dark.

"Only I succeeded," Helen said with a satisfied smile. "You won't."

Lizzie gasped. Did Jared know he was engaged to a pit viper?

"Isn't that what you always suspected?" Helen continued.

Maybe in her darkest moments, but Lizzie hadn't wanted to give the other woman that much credit. But now that Helen mentioned it... no. The idea was preposterous. Lizzie's troubles with Jared stemmed from differences of opinion about their business.

And about Lizzie's manner and dress and friends and...

Why can't you be more like Helen? Jared's exasperated query echoed through her memories.

She regarded the cool blonde in a new light. "Actually, Helen, I had you figured for more class than that."

"You always were naive."

"*Why* are you provoking me like this?" a stunned Lizzie asked. "You—Jared needs my help. Insulting me isn't the way to get it."

Helen lifted one shoulder. "So leave."

Lizzie nearly did, then thought better of it. "I would, but it'll annoy you more if I stay."

"True, but don't think staying will do you any good."

Lizzie leaned against the coffin and watched as Helen gathered up the lunch things. "Still, I think I'll stick around and see this project through."

"Then we'll have to make sure it's completed as fast as possible." Helen's smile was cold and soulless, and it made Lizzie pity her former husband.

"You're not in love with Jared, are you?" Lizzie spoke impulsively and for a moment, she didn't think Helen would respond.

"Of course not." Helen rocked back on her heels. "And he's not in love with me, either."

"Then *why* do you want to marry him?" *And why does he want to marry you?*

With a graceful movement, Helen got to her feet. "I'm very fond of Jared. After all, I've known him more than half my life. We come from the same background—" she paused, subtly emphasizing that fact "—and our families are thrilled."

Lizzie didn't doubt that. In fact she was surprised Mrs. Rutledge hadn't insisted the wedding take place immediately. "But that isn't any reason to get married."

"It's the perfect reason to get married. We have mutual friends and interests, and we do make an attractive couple."

Lizzie listened with horrified fascination. *Her* Jared would *never* have agreed to such a cold-blooded arrangement. It sounded like something from another century! "But you don't love each other."

Helen gave a hollow laugh. "When the . . . *flames* of passion burn out—and they always do—what are you left with?"

Lizzie's mouth opened and closed, but she couldn't think of an answer.

"What were you and Jared left with?"

"I . . ."

"Arguing. Fighting. Hurting each other." Helen began to pace. "Jared has had enough, and I don't have either the time or the emotional energy to go through that."

"It doesn't have to be like—"

Helen whirled to face her. "I already *have* love and passion in my life. My music. It means everything to me. Music *is* my life."

"I repeat, why get married?"

Helen crossed her arms. "Convenience. Companionship. Children."

"Ah, yes, the three Cs."

"Four. Conductors. For some reason, every conductor I've met feels it's his manly duty to make a pass at female guest artists. Marriage to Jared will allow me to refuse without bruising their colossal egos."

The conversation had an unreal quality that Lizzie couldn't blame on their surroundings. "Can't you just say no?"

"Oh, sure. Then during the performance, the tempos are off, entrances are late or early and the orchestra generally steps on your artistic toes."

"In other words, you don't make beautiful music together."

"Exactly."

Lizzie pushed away from the coffin. "Helen, I am in awe of the resourceful solution you found for your career woes. Disgusted, but awed."

"You have no right to judge me."

"No, but I will anyway. What does Jared get out of all this?"

"Me," Helen said simply.

Lizzie blinked. "What a bargain."

The room darkened as Jared filled the doorway, blocking what little light seeped inside.

It's none of your business. It's none of your business, Lizzie repeated to herself. But how could she watch Helen use Jared this way? Was he even aware of Helen's feelings—or lack of feelings? Had he actually agreed to such a calculated arrangement?

Wait a minute. Jared never got involved with anything or anyone unless he wanted to. Helen wouldn't have fooled him for an instant.

The thought depressed Lizzie.

"It seems that no carpenters are available." Jared's mouth thinned. "And I have a design too complex for my volunteers to build."

"I *told* you I'd—"

"I know where there're some carpenters," Helen interrupted.

"Where?" both Lizzie and Jared spoke at the same time.

"My parents are building a cabana next to the pool. A crew has been there all week. Use them."

It sounded good to Lizzie. She held her breath as Jared stared thoughtfully at Helen.

"Helen, that's a lovely gesture," he said at last. "But I can't use your parents' building crew."

"Why not?" Helen asked. "Mom and Dad won't be back from Vail for a month. They won't care if their cabana is delayed."

Privately, Lizzie suspected that Helen's parents had intentionally scheduled the noisy building during a time they'd be gone, but she wasn't about to mention it. She could also see that Jared was tempted to accept Helen's offer. "Better to seek forgiveness than ask permission," she said and smiled demurely.

Jared's half smile told her he remembered their motto. For a brief moment his eyes gleamed, and Lizzie felt the heady rush she used to experience when they began a new project.

Then Jared looked at Helen, and Lizzie remembered where she was. "All right, Helen, why don't you give them a call?"

"Now?" Helen's eyes slid from Jared to Lizzie.

"Yeah. Elizabeth and I have to firm up these plans."

Helen nodded stiffly, then picked up the food hamper and lifted her cheek for Jared's goodbye kiss.

He touched his lips to her cheek. Helen gazed at Lizzie for long seconds before walking out of the haunted house. Jared had already turned away and was studying Lizzie's plans.

Was this what he wanted for the rest of his life? No passion? No sizzle? No sparks?

Once she recovered from the shock of Helen's conversation, Lizzie began to simmer.

How insulting. Helen had implied that Jared's marriage to Lizzie had been such a hideous experience he didn't want to risk another of its sort.

He couldn't despise her that much, could he?

"What's the Hall of Frames?" He pointed to her sketches. "That wasn't in the Dungeon of Doom we toured, was it?"

His eyes never left the blueprints in front of him.

"Jared," she said quietly. "I had a very interesting talk with Helen. Are you in love with her?"

A muscle in his jaw jumped. "Tell me about the Hall of Frames."

"I don't want to talk about—"

Jared closed his eyes. "The Hall of Frames," he enunciated through clenched teeth.

"Portraits of normal people change to monsters in special lighting. Last picture contains a live person who shouts... Jared! Look at me."

He sighed heavily. "Elizabeth, don't say anything we'll both regret."

"You can't marry Helen."

Now he looked at her. "I can and I will."

"Don't be stupid."

"What do you care?"

"I care!" she blurted out. "I've always cared. You were the one who stopped caring."

Jared hunched over the skeleton's coffin. "That's not true," he said in a low voice. When he met her eyes, his were sad. He reached out and ran a finger lightly over the bridge of her nose. "Things just didn't pan out for us, kiddo."

She hated the sound of finality in his voice. "How could they with Helen and your parents lined up against us?"

"That's enough." Jared straightened. "I want the final plans drafted and sent to me by tomorrow."

Oh, he was so stubborn! "Fine," Lizzie snarled and rolled up her drawings. "Rather than flying to Houston and expressing these back, I'll spend the night in Dallas. May I use your office to draft these?"

"Certainly."

Lizzie shoved the drawings into the tube and fit on the cap. "See ya later."

Jared nodded dismissively.

A vision of him kissing Helen popped into her mind. So Jared was going to marry the little schemer, was he? Maybe he needed a reminder of what he'd be giving up.

Lizzie moved forward until she was nearly touching him and stopped.

"What is it?" He hopped backward.

"Aren't you going to kiss *me* goodbye?"

"No."

"Afraid?" she taunted.

Jared's eyes narrowed. "Uninterested."

Lizzie gasped softly at the pain she felt. And she believed him, until she saw the quickly masked concern that flashed across his face.

She took another step forward and this time she did touch him, running her hands across his chest. "Liar," she whispered, and raised her mouth.

Jared gazed at her for endless seconds. "Elizabeth," he groaned finally, his lips descending to meet hers.

Lizzie put everything she had into that kiss. She threw her arms around Jared's neck and held him close. She molded her body to his, savoring the familiarity of him, relearning his taste. If she thought for one minute that Jared and Helen were meant for each other, she would have backed off. But they weren't.

So she didn't.

Shortly, his crutches clattered to the floor. Jared encircled her with his arms and deepened the kiss, moving his hands over her back as if reacquainting himself with her body.

This was what she'd missed, Lizzie thought, as Jared hauled her closer. The soaring, sinking, flying, falling sensation she felt when she was with him.

Did he feel it, too?

Could he live without it?

Jared gripped her once more, spasmodically, then one hand stole under her hair and grabbed a bunch of it. He pulled until Lizzie was forced to break their kiss.

Breathing heavily, they stared at each other. "No more games, Elizabeth."

Lizzie dropped her arms. "That wasn't a game. *That,*" she said, retrieving his crutches, "was a good-bye kiss."

CHAPTER SIX

THAT WOMAN WAS DRIVING him crazy.

What had possessed him to think they could work together? Jared asked himself, as Elizabeth changed the location of the trap doors for the second time. They hadn't been able to work together when they were married; how could he expect them to do so now?

She was around all the time. He'd thought she'd give him a set of plans and go off and haunt somebody else's house. But no. No detail was too minute for her personal attention.

Why had she picked now to become a perfectionist? She hadn't been a perfectionist when they'd been partners. That was his job, and he had...well, perfected it.

"Jared, roll me over the dungeon scare again." Elizabeth plopped herself into his discarded wheelchair.

Jared, who still wore a cast, but no longer needed crutches, grabbed the back of the chair. "Elizabeth, do we have time for this modification?"

She looked up at him and batted her big blue eyes. "But *you* said it was hard to roll on these wooden boards."

"Hard, but not impossible. Let's leave them."

"Push."

"You ought to be propelling yourself."

"But I haven't had the practice at it. Roll me the speed you think the others will go."

Arguing with her only wasted time. Had Elizabeth always been this stubborn?

Jared pushed her over the dungeon scare. As originally designed, the floorboards were spaced several inches apart revealing "fire" and shadowy figures. Infrared sensors triggered the screams of prisoners. Elizabeth wanted to fill in the spaces and cut grates in the side to allow a smoother surface for the wheelchairs.

"Edward!" she bellowed, leaping out of the wheelchair.

And that was another thing, Jared griped to himself. That pale blond apprentice of Elizabeth's plainly adored her. He never disagreed with her. Anything she said was wonderful, fabulous... brilliant. Elizabeth appeared oblivious to his adoration.

"Yes, Lizzie?" Edward presented himself, pencil at the ready.

"If I cut grates there—" she pointed "—and there, how will it affect the backstage areas for the actors?"

"I'll check on it at once."

Jared half expected him to clink his heels and salute.

Edward opened one of the wooden panels forming the wall of the corridor and disappeared inside. When in place, the panel concealed the entrance.

"Elizabeth," Jared spoke in a low voice, "just fill in the gaps and skip this scare."

She squatted down. "What? You mean *simplify* the design, Jared?"

She was really enjoying this. All right, he hadn't realized what his insistence that she not change anything would involve.

But he wasn't ready to tell her so. "I'm concerned about finishing on time."

"Aren't we all," Elizabeth replied as a muffled thumping sounded from behind the wall. "Where are you, Edward?"

Edward thumped again.

Elizabeth thumped back.

At last they decided on the size and position of the grates.

Jared wanted to sit down. His leg felt heavy, and the breeze from the fans running inside the partially built house didn't reach to the center, where they were now.

Sweat trickled down his back. The skin under his cast itched. The fumes from the fire-retardant paint irritated his nose.

And Elizabeth looked like she'd just been to an aerobics class. She wore skintight bicycle shorts and a cropped tank top, neon running shoes and an armful of bracelets. Every taut curve was on display. Helen would never wear such a provocative outfit.

He shouldn't even notice Elizabeth's attire, let alone her curves.

Suddenly he hoped for a cold front. It was the second week in October; wasn't it about time for one?

"Edward, make the changes on the plans and remember to add backing or the operator will be visible."

"Will do," replied Edward's muffled voice.

"There." Elizabeth got to her feet. "Any other questions?"

"Yes. The Hall of Frames." Jared gestured for her to precede him.

The wheelchair was in the way. Instead of moving it, Elizabeth squeezed between the wheelchair and Jared.

Very slowly and very close to him.

The warm spicy scent she wore teased him. He closed his eyes and inhaled. No other woman in his acquaintance had ever worn perfume like it. It was uniquely Elizabeth.

It was fall and pumpkin pie and cinnamon and apple cider. It was caramel apples, vanilla sugar cookies and cloves.

It wasn't Helen. Helen smelled like roses.

"Are you all right?"

Jared opened his eyes to find Elizabeth looking up at him through her lashes. "Yes." But he wasn't all right. He hadn't been all right since they'd kissed.

That kiss had been a monumental mistake he had no intention of repeating. No matter how much he wanted to.

"You look tired." Teasing Jared was no fun if he couldn't fully appreciate it. "How about lunch?"

"Lunch is a wonderful idea."

He sounded so enthusiastic that Lizzie thought his foot must be bothering him. Just like a man not to admit pain when he felt it.

"Edward!" Lizzie shouted. "Where are you now?"

"Still in the dungeon scare," was Edward's muffled reply.

"Come out of there. You'll roast."

"I'm measuring."

Jared knocked against the wall. "It's okay to finish after lunch."

A flushed Edward emerged, sweat trickling down the sides of his face. "Thanks. Remind me to note the changes before I leave this afternoon. I'm going to inspect the Hall of Frames now, then I'll grab a bite to eat." He disappeared farther into the house.

"Shall I call out for pizza?" Lizzie asked Jared as they walked single file through the twisting corridors toward the entrance.

"Only if you'll allow me to eat pepperoni in peace," Jared replied.

"It's loaded with fat."

"That's why I like pepperoni."

"Ick." Lizzie glanced over her shoulder at him. "Have you had your cholesterol checked lately?"

"It won't matter because I'm going to eat what I want anyway."

"Figures." At the next corner Lizzie hopped over the light beam that triggered the sound effects. Hearing the groans and roars all the time irritated her, but it was too much trouble to disconnect them.

Jared grinned and walked through the sensor, setting off the howls and screams. When Lizzie rolled her eyes at him, he threw back his head and laughed.

It was the first uninhibited laugh she'd heard from Jared in a long, long while. It brought back memories of happier times and a more relaxed Jared. The Jared he'd been before they'd begun their own business.

Responding to the twinkle in his eyes, Lizzie ran back through the sensor herself. Jared moved on ahead, and Lizzie heard moaning from the next startle area. Jared was tripping the sound effects there. Giggling, she answered with her howls; he responded with more moans. They were louder than she remembered and even seemed to be coming closer.

What a great effect. Intrigued, she abandoned her howls and screams and walked toward the moaning. She rounded a corner and ran smack into a solid, warm but not furry body.

It moaned.

Lizzie yelped a split second before she recognized Jared.

"Gotcha!" Jared laughed demonically and hunched over her.

Feeling rather chagrined, Lizzie laughed with him, giving him a playful shove as they entered the skeleton's crypt.

"Hey, watch it!" Jared said. "I'm still recovering here."

"You pull any more stunts like that and you'll have a relapse," Lizzie threatened with a mock scowl.

"If you two have finished playing, you can eat now," said a disapproving voice.

"Helen!" Abruptly, the old Jared vanished.

"I thought I'd save you time and bring lunch." Helen gestured to the folding chairs and card table set with a checkered cloth and coordinating napkins. "I was under the impression that time was critical."

"It is," he confirmed mildly.

Helen's gaze flicked between Lizzie and Jared.

It was an awkward moment that Lizzie decided to ignore. Seating herself at the table, she whisked a napkin onto her lap and took a long swallow of iced tea. "Tastes wonderful," she said with a bland look at the other two.

"I thought we'd be cooler with the table set in front of the fan. You won't be too cold, will you, Elizabeth?" she asked with a pointed inspection of Lizzie's skimpy attire.

Lizzie favored her with a wide smile and dug into her salad. "Nope. I'm fine."

Jared held out a chair for Helen, and she slipped onto it, her head held stiffly.

Except for the hum of the box fan, the room was deadly quiet. Appropriate for a crypt, but rather inhibiting for a luncheon.

Lizzie rattled her bangles just to make some noise. Helen sniffed.

Jared stared at his salad with an unreadable expression on his face. If Lizzie didn't know better, she'd suspect that he was struggling not to laugh.

"So." Helen took a sip of her tea. "Is the construction proceeding according to schedule?"

"Yes and no," Jared replied.

When Helen raised a delicately arched brow, he continued. "Elizabeth has modified some sections—"

"Oh, *has* she?" Helen narrowed her eyes.

"Improvements, Helen," Jared said gently.

"Need I remind you that the house must open in two weeks?" Helen snapped.

"No," Lizzie answered cheerfully, "but you probably will anyway."

Jared cleared his throat and shot Lizzie a sharp look. "We're lucky that the construction crew at Helen's parents' home was willing to delay that job and take on this one."

"Just trying to do my part." Helen gave him a proprietary pat on his arm.

"We're *all* doing our part," Lizzie said in a hearty voice.

"Yes, but some of us are doing it faster than others."

Lizzie wanted to wipe that smug smile off Helen's face. "Listen, I—" She began, ready to tell Helen exactly how heavy her own schedule was, when Jared kicked her. Lizzie was surprised into silence.

Once again, Helen had managed to provoke her, making Lizzie seem like a hothead.

Of course, Lizzie *was* a hothead, but Helen was extremely provoking.

And anyway, Lizzie and Jared weren't married anymore, so if he wanted to kick somebody, why didn't he kick that conniving fiancée of his?

Lizzie had suffered years of Helen's sly remarks and digs. She'd never complained about them. Somehow, she'd always thought that Jared would notice—if he truly loved her.

He never had.

Looking at him now, Lizzie saw the censuring gaze she'd been the recipient of so many times in the past. She raised her chin defiantly.

At that moment, the room darkened as a bronzed, shirtless, heavily muscled man appeared in the doorway. He balanced an ice chest on his shoulder. "Where do you want this, Ms. Travis?"

Helen pointed. "Just inside the doorway, Rico. Thanks." The smile she gave him was friendlier than any she'd ever given Lizzie.

Pectorals rippling, Rico swung the ice chest to the ground. He turned to leave, then stopped, one hand propped on the door jamb. "Ms. Wilcox? Edward says to tell you he's ready to leave. He wants to talk to you for a minute."

"Where is he?"

Rico wiped sweat from his forehead with the back of his hand. "That place with the pictures."

"Tell him I'll be right there," Lizzie said.

Rico nodded, flashed a quick look at Helen and left.

For the next several seconds, Helen stared after him.

Lizzie made a face, then crumpled her napkin and dropped it beside her plate. "If you'll excuse me, I'm going to see what Edward has to say about the Hall of Frames."

Edward was concerned about wheelchairs gouging the orange wallpaper decorating the hall. He had a point. Lizzie was trying to decide between painting the lower part of the hallway black or leaving it papered when Jared hobbled into view.

"I don't understand why you put wallpaper here anyway," he commented.

"It's supposed to look like an ordinary house. Also, the hallway is brighter and disorients people when they run from here to the pitch-black area that's next."

Jared nodded absently, then squatted to the floor. "May I borrow your pen?" he asked.

Lizzie handed him the pen she'd stuck behind her ear while she conferred with Edward. The wallpaper would stay as it was.

Moments later, Edward left for the airport, and she turned back to Jared. "Is Helen still here?"

"No." Jared was forcing the pen down the inside of his cast. "She's off to rehearse with the Plano symphony."

Goody, Lizzie thought. The less she and Helen saw of one another, the better.

"I can't wait for this cast to come off. It itches like crazy." He bent over his leg. Since he wore shorts, quite a lot of his leg was visible.

Jared had nice legs for a man and his recent lack of exercise hadn't visibly affected them. Golden brown hair dusted perpetually golden brown skin. Lizzie had always envied Jared's natural honey skin tone, what with tanning being bad for people now. Not that she'd ever tanned. She remained glowing white, except for the freckles that sprinkled her skin like cinnamon on whipped cream.

Jared rubbed at the edge of his cast, the contrast of it against his leg reminding her of her skin against—

She closed her eyes and swallowed. She should never have kissed him. She didn't need to be reminded that the one place she and Jared were perfectly and gloriously compatible was the bedroom.

"No sleeping on the job."

She did *not* feel sleepy. "I had a short lunch break."

Lizzie sat next to Jared and watched the play of muscles in his back as he twisted the pen inside his cast.

She remembered what those muscles felt like. How many times had she massaged his neck and shoulders after he'd spent hours drawing?

And how many times had those massages led to— *Stop it!*

Lizzie tore her gaze away from Jared. She was making herself...miserable was one way to describe it. "Why are you marrying Helen?"

"None of your business."

"It's my business when I get kicked because of her."

"You were about to pick on her." He looked up briefly. "She did provide the carpenters."

"Her parents did," Lizzie grumbled under her breath.

"So *your* grandiose haunted house could be built in time."

"*My* grandiose house? It's benefiting *your* clinic."

"And *your* reputation."

Lizzie inhaled and exhaled twice before replying, "For *your* information, if any house will make my reputation, it will be the Haunted Hotel in the ghost town that's being built near Richmond."

"How impressive." Jared made a derisive sound. "The highlight of your career is building a haunted hotel in a fake ghost town."

Lizzie gritted her teeth. "There is slightly more to it than that."

"How much more can there be?"

"This will be a permanent structure, for one thing," she said, thinking that would impress him. Jared was big on permanency.

"You said *this* house would be permanent," he pointed out.

"I mean it will be open all year. They're trying to expand tourism in the area. There's already a functioning ranch and a weekend rodeo. The ghost town will have several buildings filled with Old West memorabilia. My Haunted Hotel will provide the amusement." She could tell that Jared still wasn't impressed. "I'll receive a percentage of the ticket sales."

Lizzie considered this commission a major career milestone. For the first time since she'd started her own firm, she'd have a small, but steady income. And with any luck, the income wouldn't be that small. "The grand opening is on Halloween," she added, just so Jared would know how much of a favor she was doing for him.

"I hope it works out for you." His voice was completely devoid of enthusiasm.

More hurt by his indifference than she cared to admit, Lizzie lashed out. "And I hope your marriage works out for you."

"Thank you." He politely returned her pen.

"But I don't think it has a ghost of a chance."

"I learn from my mistakes." He gazed at her steadily, letting his meaning sink in.

"You're going to be very well-educated."

"Elizabeth!"

"You're not in love with each other, Helen told me so, herself!"

Jared stared at her for a long moment. "There are many kinds of love."

"Don't give me that!" Lizzie slammed the orange wall behind her with her fist.

Jared took her hand and unclenched the fingers. "Elizabeth...when our marriage was good, it was very, very good." Sadness tinged his smile. "But when it was bad..." He trailed off, shaking his head. "I can't go through that again."

Lizzie snatched her hand away. "Did you ever try to figure out just what exactly went wrong with our marriage?"

Jared's lips thinned. "We're too different—"

"That's your mother talking. That's Helen talking. I can just hear what she said after I left."

"She said nothing against you."

Lizzie groaned and looked toward the ceiling. Men—particularly Jared—could be so obtuse. "Of course she didn't. That's not the way she operates. Jared, she was at your door not five minutes after I pulled out of the driveway."

"You are, as usual, exaggerating."

"I'm not!" Lizzie jumped to her feet and began to pace. "I know for a fact. I came back—"

"You came back?" The strangled tone in his voice stopped her in midstride.

"For...for my mechanical pencil."

"For your pencil." Something flickered and died in his eyes.

"The one you gave me for Christmas."

"But I mailed it to you—you didn't come back for that."

Lizzie gestured impotently. "Helen was there."

Jared stared at her, then gazed sightlessly ahead. "You hurt me by leaving. A lot."

"It hurt to leave."

"Then why did you?" He shot the question at her, as if he'd wanted to ask it for a long time.

Lizzie sighed and leaned against the wall. "Because you changed—and I expected you to," she said quickly to forestall his protest. "I expected to grow and change, too. But I thought we'd grow closer, not further apart."

His brows knit together and, he appeared to be considering her words. Maybe she finally had his attention. Maybe they could finally talk without accusations and tears. "Remember how it was when your parents still lived in Dallas, before they retired to Sweetwater?"

He shrugged. "I suppose we did see them a lot. But my father had connections in the construction industry. We were just starting out and needed the contacts."

Lizzie decided not to point out that only one of those contacts had resulted in a commission. The rest of their clients had come from their apprenticeship days and her haunted house designs. "True. But what I remember was desperately trying to fit in with your parents' friends. I never could get it right, dress right—"

"I heard my mother offer to take you shopping."

Lizzie squeezed her eyes shut. "Please." The humiliating offer had been made during a luncheon in front of

Helen and her mother and several other condescending matrons. Lizzie's flower print dress had been out-powered by the shoulder pads in style at the time. She'd gone country girl; they'd gone "Dynasty."

And she hadn't even liked her dress to begin with. She'd thought sweet and demure was what Mrs. Rut-ledge wanted in a daughter-in-law.

"Jared, the point is that *I* did all the changing. I tried to become what *you* wanted. I haven't traveled like you have, and my family isn't a member of the same social circles that your family is. I'm no country bumpkin, yet, when I'm with your mother and Helen, that's the way I feel. I tried so hard for their approval that I became someone I didn't even recognize."

"I had no idea—"

"*I know.*" Lizzie slid down the wall until she sat next to Jared again. "If you'd taken my side even once, I might have been able to stand it."

"I still thing you're exaggerating...."

Lizzie shook her head. "In your mother's eyes, my biggest flaw is that I'm not Helen. *You* even tried to turn me into Helen."

"No." But it was more of an automatic protest. Lizzie could see that Jared was sifting through memories.

"Yes. Helen this and Helen that and why can't you be more like Helen...? Well, Jared, now that you've got Helen are you happy?"

CHAPTER SEVEN

"YOU GO IN FIRST and make sure she's decent."

"The poor thing's always decent."

A male guffaw was quickly stifled.

"Shh! You'll wake her up," cautioned a motherly voice.

"I thought that's why we were standing outside her door."

"She needs the sleep."

That's right, so go away, Lizzie thought and snuggled deeper into the sofa pillows as the door opened.

"Then why doesn't she sleep at night? It's almost noon."

"Noon!" Lizzie shouted and bolted upright, scrambling for her watch. "It can't be noon! Carleen, why didn't you wake me up?"

The older woman sagged against Edward, hands crossed over her heart. "Lizzie...you scared me half to death."

"Yeah." Edward peered at her. "She does look pretty scary right now."

Lizzie found her watch, which confirmed that it was indeed approaching noon. She sighed and sank back into the couch pillows. "Great. Just great." She finger combed her frizzy curls, trying to fluff out the side she'd slept on. "What did I miss?"

"About twenty-five phone calls from your ex," Edward told her, pushing his wire-rimmed glasses against the bridge of his nose.

"Edward," admonished Carleen.

Lizzie hid a smile.

"The guy won't talk with me. He insists on talking to *Elizabeth*." Edward dropped his voice in imitation of Jared. "I told him you weren't available but he phones every fifteen minutes. I can't get anything done, and *she's*—" he jerked a thumb toward Carleen "—on the other line all the time."

Lizzie looked toward Carleen. "Who else called?"

Carleen bustled around the room, straightening up. "The Haunted Hotel people have the county inspector coming out this afternoon and want you to be there. The Dungeon of Doom has developed lighting problems. The Richardson Mall people want to know if you're available for publicity photos—"

Lizzie held up her hands. "Okay. Give me a minute."

Carleen opened the miniblinds. Lizzie winced as sunlight stabbed her grainy eyes. "Is there any coffee downstairs?"

"Yes, and it ought to be good and strong by now," Edward said, sprinting off to fetch it.

Carleen shook her head at Lizzie and disappeared into the bedroom with Lizzie's clutter.

"Elizabeth Wilcox, when was the last time you did your laundry?"

Lizzie rested her head on her knees. "It's okay, Carleen," she said, wearily.

"No, it is not!" Carleen returned, bearing an armful of Lizzie's underwear. "I'll run this load downstairs for you."

"Carleeeen! Not during office hours!" Lizzie moaned. "Please don't drag my dirty underwear past Edward."

"I saw all your underwear last year." Edward had reappeared with her coffee.

"A gentleman wouldn't have mentioned it," Lizzie grumbled, taking the cup from him.

"It was no big thrill." Edward collapsed next to her on the sofa and tossed a calendar on the low table in front of them. "Seriously, Liz." She always became Liz when Edward wanted to be serious. "Our schedule is the most frightening thing I've seen."

"I told you it would be." He wasn't about to quit, was he? He couldn't quit. She'd cry if she had to and the way she felt, she wouldn't even have to fake it.

"I know. And at the beginning of the season, we had all our projects booked. The schedule was heavy, but doable. Then you added that house for your ex—"

"His name is Jared."

"Well, *Jared* is demanding triple the time of any other project."

"I know." Lizzie sipped her coffee. "That's the way we used to work together. It's an old habit."

"Break it." Edward grabbed the calendar and plopped it on her lap. "We have final inspections due."

"I'm aware of that." Lizzie spoke rather sternly. Casual they might be, but Edward was her employee and, though she'd be in trouble if he quit now, she wasn't going to have him tell her how to run her business.

He raised his eyebrows, obviously hearing and correctly interpreting her tone. "Okay," he said slowly. "I was merely going to suggest—just suggest, mind you— that I do the Lubbock inspection. It'll be a two-day trip, and you've got a lot on your plate right now."

Lizzie nodded, sighing. "Sorry to snap at you."

His suggestion made sense, but Lizzie had always done all the final inspections herself. She liked to see how the house looked, took pictures for her files and generally dispensed tips for crowd control and flow. In fact, it was her favorite part.

But this was Edward's second Halloween with her. He was perfectly capable of performing the final inspections, and he had a valid point. Jared was demanding too much of her time.

"Okay, Edward. You do the Lubbock inspection," she said with reluctance. "And take lots of pictures."

"Yes!" Edward shook a fist in the air. "I'll call them and make arrangements for it right now. And as long as I'm there, what about Santa Fe?" When she nodded her assent, he jumped off the couch, grabbed his calendar and went out the door.

"Tell Carleen I'm coming down to check my messages," Lizzie called after him.

Considerably more time elapsed than she would have liked before she made her way downstairs.

Carleen was just hanging up the telephone. With a look at Lizzie, she carefully ripped off a piece of pumpkin-shaped paper and added it to a growing pile.

"Need I ask who that was?"

Carleen removed her rhinestone cat eyeglasses and leaned back in her chair. "He suggested you get a pager."

Lizzie perched on the corner of Carleen's desk and riffled through the messages. As Edward had said, most were from Jared.

"You'd think he'd never built anything by himself before," sniffed Carleen.

"No. It's just that Jared likes to be involved in every step of the building process. Since this is my design, he wants to make sure I'm on top of things."

Carleen tapped one rhinestone cat tail against the side of her mouth. "He's an architect. You both don't have to be there all the time."

Lizzie sorted her messages into two stacks. "He never liked to delegate much."

"Then why don't you delegate to him?"

Lizzie didn't meet Carleen's eyes. Instead, she shoved one message stack across the desk.

"It sounds as if the two of you are making excuses to see each other."

"Don't be silly," Lizzie mumbled. "He's engaged."

"And having second thoughts, no doubt."

"Jared? Admit he made a mistake? He hates admitting he made a mistake almost as much as he hates making one. Believe me, I know." She slid off Carleen's desk. "Each time I'm in Dallas, I keep hoping he'll say something like 'there *is* more to designing haunted houses than I thought' or 'what you do *is* important.'"

"He had to call you for help, didn't he?"

Lizzie paced in front of Carleen's desk. "I can't understand why he involved himself with a haunted house anyway. Did I ever tell you that I almost gave up designing haunted houses because he thought they were tacky?"

"But they're beautiful designs," protested the loyal Carleen. "They're just as difficult to design as other architectural structures. You follow safety regulations, your plans are professional and you oversee the construction like any other architect would. What's tacky about them?"

"They're commercial and appeal to the masses."

"So?"

"Anything that appeals to the hoi polloi will never appear in those snooty architectural magazines. Jared wants to design for the ages. I want to design for love and money."

Carleen put on her cat eyeglasses and read the stack of messages Lizzie had left on her desk. "So why didn't you each design what you wanted and leave the other alone?"

Lizzie stopped pacing. "We tried, but Jared hated the fact that Rutledge and Wilcox was known for haunted house designs. He didn't want anything to do with haunted houses."

"Well, he's obviously changed his mind."

"Yeah." Lizzie sighed and walked toward the stairs. "Call and reserve a seat on the three o'clock flight to Dallas, okay?"

"Lizzie!"

Lizzie dangled one of the pumpkin messages. "Richardson Mall publicity pictures, remember?"

Carleen snatched up the phone. "If you insist on going, then put on some makeup. You're starting to resemble a corpse."

"ELIZABETH, YOU LOOK dead on your feet."

"Thank you very much!" It didn't help that Jared looked his usual suave self, from his freshly trimmed hair to the crease in his pants. Lizzie felt limp and rumpled.

She jerked open the door of Jared's Mercedes and collapsed onto the soft leather seat. The publicity photos and interview had taken longer than she'd thought. For the last half hour, she'd been acutely conscious of

Jared waiting by his car, checking his watch every five minutes. *I do love my work. I do love my work. I do, I do, I do love my work.* Jared shut her door and walked, limping slightly, around the car to the driver's side. "What time do you have to be back at the airport?"

Lizzie closed her eyes. "Last flight's at eight-thirty."

Jared said something, but it was too much trouble to ask him to repeat it. Her seat was so comfortable and the air-conditioning so refreshing. . . .

Jared was shaking her shoulder. "Elizabeth, we're here."

"Huh?" She opened her eyes and found they were sitting in the parking lot at the Hanes Memorial Haunted House. "But you just started the car!" Her head felt full and fuzzy.

"You conked out almost immediately." A devilish smile played about his lips. "You still snore."

"Amazing. Even asleep, I manage to annoy you." Lizzie pushed open the car door and banged it shut, the vibrations echoing in her head.

It was dusk and the house looked appropriately spooky. She heard Jared's door close and waited for him to join her. "Don't forget to hang ghosts in the tree there." She pointed to the lone oak between the clinic and the house. "Also clear out anything that might trip people around the exits. They move pretty fast."

"Okay." Jared made a note. "You'll be back up here, though."

The tone of his voice rubbed Lizzie the wrong way. "I don't have time to keep flying up here to baby-sit your carpenters."

"And I don't have time to attend your press conferences," he snapped. "You aren't the only one who's running a business."

"And how many monuments have you designed lately?"

The headlights of an approaching car illuminated his tight-lipped face. "For your information, I've just learned that I'm one of two architects being considered for the contract on the new Whitaker Contemporary Art Gallery. It'll be standing long after your structures have been razed."

"Congratulations." It was what he'd always wanted. "I hope you get it."

"So do I." He didn't sound terribly optimistic.

"What's wrong?"

Jared raked his hair with his fingers in an uncharacteristic display of frustration. "How do you think my involvement with *this*—" he gestured his contempt "—is going to look to the selection committee?"

Lizzie froze, her lips parted.

In the distance, a car door slammed.

At her silence, Jared glanced down, wincing when he saw her face. "Elizabeth . . . I'm sorry."

Lizzie swallowed. "No, you're not. You've always felt that way about haunted houses." She saw his wary expression and scoffed, "Don't worry. I'm much too professional to leave you in the lurch."

She stalked toward the entrance. Jared's attitude was no surprise, but her reaction was. She hurt. Still.

"Elizabeth." He caught up with her and reached for her arm. She'd forgotten that he could walk faster now. "I *am* sorry. It was a thoughtless remark."

"I'll get over it." But it would take a while.

Jared slowly slid his hand down her arm. They stood in the deepening twilight.

"I haven't given you enough credit," he said at last. "You do take your job seriously and I respect that."

Lizzie managed a small smile. At last he—

"Jared? Is Elizabeth with you?"

Helen. Her timing was as perfect as everything else.

"Yes. Helen," he answered. "We were supposed to meet for dinner," he explained to Lizzie.

Did Lizzie detect a trace of irritation in his voice?

Helen, exquisitely attired in raw silk, approached them. "Elizabeth, when I went by Jared's office, they told me your office had been trying to locate you. Something about a haunted hotel?"

"What about it?" Lizzie asked sharply.

"Apparently someone was hurt during a walk-through, and they want you to make modifications immediately."

"Oh, no." Lizzie slumped against the rough outside wall of Jared's house. "Was it serious?"

Helen shook her head. "Your secretary didn't say."

Lizzie brightened. "Then it wasn't serious. Carleen would have gone into detail. She loves gore." Straightening, she said, "Jared, let's make this a quickie. I need to get to the airport."

"Sure." Jared took her elbow in one hand and Helen's in the other.

But of course, there was nothing quick about it.

Jared studied the plans. "So we'll widen this hall, right?"

Lizzie nodded wearily. "Shorten the wall here so the corner won't be as sharp. I didn't realize how difficult it was to maneuver wheelchairs, and I don't want people clogging up there." She reached for the blueprints.

"I'll put in the modifications."

Lizzie hesitated, then acquiesced. Without knowing precisely what was wrong with the Haunted Hotel, she ought to accept whatever help he offered.

"Halloween is next week. What will these changes do to our schedule?" Helen asked.

"We're already behind." Jared shrugged. "More overtime for the carpenters."

As if she didn't already feel bad enough, Lizzie thought. At least things couldn't get any worse.

"I'll tell you what," Helen announced. "*I'll* help. Rico—he's the head carpenter—can show me how to pound nails or something."

"That's awfully nice of you, Helen, but..." Lizzie looked to Jared for support. Helen messing with the carpenters. That's all they needed.

"Sure," Jared said, to Lizzie's surprise. "Talk to Rico tomorrow. He'll find something for you to do."

Nope. Things couldn't get any worse.

THINGS GOT WORSE.

"I don't think you should go up there. She might be asleep."

A male voice argued with Carleen. Who was it? Not Edward, he wasn't due back from the site inspections for a couple of days. Lizzie tried to call out, but a rasping croak was all she could manage.

Footsteps sounded on the stairs. She hunched down on the sofa, drawing her comforter up to her chin. What a doozy of a cold.

The door burst open, and Jared came in, a disapproving Carleen fluttered behind him.

Hands resting on his hips, he stared down at Lizzie.

"There. Now do you believe me?" Carleen grabbed Lizzie's empty glass and headed for the kitchen.

Lizzie sniffed and tried to look pathetic, which wasn't hard.

"How could you do this to yourself?" Jared demanded.

It wouldn't kill him to show some sympathy. "It was easy. I stood on a street corner and flagged down a passing virus."

"She exhausted herself taking on an extra job as a favor for somebody," sniped Carleen from the kitchen. "Lizzie, do you want chicken noodle or vegetable beef soup?"

"Chicken noodle," Jared answered for her. "She'll pick out the carrots in the other one."

"Too mushy," mumbled Lizzie.

Jared shoved her legs aside and sat on the sofa, propping his cast on her coffee table. "I guess this means you aren't going to fly back with me and see the changes we've made on the house."

"No, she is not!" Carleen banged a saucepan, emphasizing her point.

"You two carry on. I'm going back to sleep." Lizzie pulled the comforter over her head.

She heard rustling.

"What's all this?"

When she peeked over the edge of the comforter, Lizzie saw Jared gathering scattered drawings for the Haunted Hotel from around the sofa. Wincing, he moved his foot to the floor and spread the drawings out on the table. "What're you trying to do here?"

Lizzie wiggled upright, clutching the sofa back as a slight dizziness overtook her. When it passed, she explained, "Apparently the exit sign above that door wasn't operating. The electrician stood on the hallway railing to have a look and fell off."

"That was stupid."

Lizzie agreed. "However, Mr. Gelfin, the manager of the ghost town, is afraid that people touring the hotel might climb on the railing, too. He's worried about being sued. I've got to figure out a way to move people from point A to point B in complete safety."

"Hmm." Jared rubbed his chin as he examined her drawings.

Lizzie watched him. She knew there was a simple solution, but her brain wasn't working very well. The hotel people had called, wondering where their plans were. They'd probably called several times, but Lizzie suspected Carleen hadn't told her.

She glanced into the kitchen where Carleen was making another pitcher of orange juice for her and smiled. Carleen had a tendency to fuss and right now, Lizzie was glad.

"Why don't you reinforce these poles and run them up to the ceiling?" Jared suggested.

"I tried that. Mr. Gelfin doesn't want anyone in that hallway."

"Then how are they supposed to get to the upstairs bedrooms?"

"That's the problem."

"I think your Mr. Gelfin is overreacting."

"Mr. Gelfin frequently overreacts."

"You two must get along wonderfully." Brow wrinkling, Jared studied the plans a moment longer. "Why don't I talk to him? He's calmed down by now, and I'll convince him that the bars are the best solution."

"You're offering to talk to one of my clients for me?"

Jared rolled up her plans, ignoring her open-mouthed astonishment. "Sure. If I don't, you'll lie there and stew instead of getting well. Then you can't come and look at my house."

Why couldn't he just be nice to be nice? "Heaven forbid something should interfere with your house."

Lizzie gazed out her window at the glorious October day and felt sorry for herself. Fat tears pooled in her eyes and rolled down her cheeks.

Why didn't Jared hurry up and leave? She sniffed and swiped at a tear. Another quickly took its place.

"Here." A box of tissues landed in her lap. "Blow your nose like a good girl."

Lizzie didn't look at him as she snatched up a tissue and blew.

Tilting her chin until she had to face him, Jared said in a gentle voice, "Don't worry, Elizabeth. Everything will be all right."

"Everything?"

He gazed at her for a long time, then took her into his arms. "Everything," he whispered.

And leaning on his broad shoulder, feeling the warmth of his arms around her, Lizzie believed him.

HALLOWEEN WAS ONLY three days away before Lizzie could return to Dallas.

Jared's phone calls had tapered off. A huge basket of smiley-faced oranges had arrived from him with a card that read, "Hope to 'C' you soon."

Jared had also sweet-talked Mr. Gelfin into accepting Lizzie's modifications for the Haunted Hotel, and she'd completed those. Edward had inspected both the Lubbock house and the one in Santa Fe. Carleen had washed all Lizzie's laundry and fortified her with frozen casseroles.

This morning, Lizzie had flown to Austin, posed for pictures and spent two hours watching people tour her house there. This afternoon, she'd paid a visit to the

Richardson Mall house and was, at last, on her way to Jared's house. She was even running early. She'd called Jared and had arranged to meet him there in about forty-five minutes.

She was nervous about seeing him again. That day in her apartment, when she'd been sick, she'd seen the old Jared. The Jared she'd married, the Jared who cared about her.

The one she'd loved.

And still loved.

What a rotten mess. It wasn't bad enough that she fell in love with him once, she'd gone and fallen in love with him all over again. It was no good telling herself that he despised her haunted house business. And her silly heart refused to listen to the memories of her strained encounters with his parents.

Lizzie pulled her rental car into the parking lot. Rico's pickup truck was also there. Good. Maybe the foreman had left the doors unlocked, and she could get started.

The grounds had been cleared. Lizzie inspected areas around the entrance and exit and decided to suggest some lighting for safety. She wore her black tennis shoes with the glow-in-the-dark skeletons painted on them. If she could see the skeletons glowing, she knew an area was too dark.

The side of the building next to the clinic was unlit, too. Just the place for unauthorized ghouls to hang out. She'd recommend that Jared hire some extra security.

She sighed. In three days, she'd have no excuse to hear Jared's voice or to hop on a plane and see him. In three days, she'd be out of his life.

Of course, she'd technically been out of his life during the past three years, but deep down, she'd refused to accept that.

Since she was near the exit, Lizzie tried the door there. As she suspected, it was unlocked. The lights were on, but the matte black walls absorbed most of the brightness, leaving a dim and gloomy interior.

Lizzie walked through the halls slowly, checking the construction of the house. As always, she stepped over the sensors to avoid triggering the irksome howls and screams.

She walked deeper into the house, examining the backstage areas and controlling the props. Lizzie had prepared a list of instructions she left with each group on her final inspection, but for Jared, she made hand-written notes.

Approaching the modified dungeon area, she opened the backstage door. This was one of the larger rooms, common to three sections of the house. It would be cramped—and hot.

Even though the weather was cooler, no air could circulate in this area.

Lizzie wrote a reminder to Jared to provide the operators with some small fans. The biggest problem was keeping them out of the way. Lizzie scanned the walls, checking for the small ledges she had suggested be installed to hold the fans.

Not there. Smiling to herself, she wrote another note. The ledges were frequently omitted by people who didn't understand their function.

Remembering Rico's truck in the parking lot, Lizzie decided to search for any carpenters still present. Maybe they could add the shelves, and she wouldn't have to bother Jared about them.

Pushing open the door opposite the one she'd entered, Lizzie stepped into the hallway outside the Cells of Lost Souls just as someone tripped the moaning sound effect. She was headed toward the room where it was located when she heard a feminine gasping that she didn't remember being in that particular recording.

Lizzie stopped.

"Don't stop," pleaded a woman.

Shrugging, Lizzie continued walking, automatically stepping over the infrared sensor at the entrance to the cells. The woman sounded almost like . . .

Helen.

"Don't tease me. I can't bear it!"

It *was* Helen. Lizzie froze in midstep as a man's rich chuckle mingled with Helen's pleading.

"Yes! Yes! I'll admit it—I love you!"

All the blood drained from Lizzie's face. As her eyes adjusted to the dim light, she saw two prone figures inside one of the cells. Helen's fair head was next to one with hair of a familiar rich sable.

"Please tell me that you love me, too!"

A masculine murmuring followed, pierced by Helen's squeals of joy. "Oh, I knew it! I knew you loved me!"

Lizzie's mouth opened in a silent scream. Love! Helen and Jared had fallen in love with each other.

Lizzie felt her heart explode leaving nothing behind but a great gaping hole.

Intellectually, Lizzie had known that Helen and Jared were engaged, but somehow, after Jared's visit when she'd been sick. . .after he'd talked to the Haunted Hotel people on her behalf. . .after the weeks of working with him, she'd thought, *hoped*—

He *couldn't* love Helen. Not that way.

As if proving otherwise, the two figures locked in an embrace.

Lizzie clutched her stomach. She was going to be sick, violently sick right here in the Cells of Lost Souls. Covering her mouth with her hand, she turned and ran.

Electronic howling and wailing reverberated through the Hanes Memorial Haunted House.

A woman screamed.

A man cursed.

Lizzie groaned. She'd tripped the sensor.

Now what? She halted in indecision, the nausea subsiding.

Wait a minute. What was she doing? She couldn't let them know that she was anything other than mildly embarrassed at stumbling across them. Helen and Jared were engaged. And no matter what her private fantasies were, she was no longer a part of Jared's personal life. It was time she accepted that. *He* obviously had.

Besides, they were bound to figure out that she was the person who'd discovered them. She should bluff her way through this and spare everybody's feelings.

Sighing, Lizzie gathered her pride and returned to the other room, setting off the sound effects again for good measure. "Don't worry, it's only me," she sang out. "I was early and thought I'd start the inspection." She listened and could hear them rustling around. "Sorry to intrude."

Lizzie studiously avoided looking inside a certain cell and instead checked various instruments of torture in the cells opposite it. The scurrying sounds stopped. She cleared her throat, her gaze trained on the concrete floor. "If everybody's decent, I wanted to show Jared the large backstage area. It needs shelves for some small fans."

No one answered. Out of the corner of her eye, Lizzie saw a pale figure emerge from the cell.

Silence.

For pity's sake, why should she have to do all the talking? Lizzie glanced up into Helen's stricken face.

"I..." Helen's eyes swiveled toward the infamous cell.

"It's okay, Helen," Lizzie hastened to reassure her. Poor Helen had probably never been at the mercy of her libido before. "I just need to talk with Jared about a couple of things and then I'll leave."

They stared at one another. Helen's pale blond hair fell loosely about her shoulders. Her cheeks were pink and her lips swollen.

Lizzie had never seen her look lovelier.

"Hurry up, Jared!" Lizzie called, hearing her voice crack. She strode to the door of the tiny room. "I've had a long—"

She broke off as she encountered a bare chest. A heavily muscled chest.

Rico's chest.

CHAPTER EIGHT

LIZZIE STARED INTO Rico's black eyes. "I, uh, I thought you were somebody else."

"I'm Rico." His voice reverberated near her ear.

"Um, yes." She floundered backward when she realized that she still stood inches away from his gleaming chest. "I see that you are."

Clearly amused, Rico stooped to retrieve his shirt. Helen was doing her ghost imitation in the far corner.

Helen and Rico.

Rico and Helen.

Jared and . . .

Jared!

What about Jared?

Her gaze flew to a wide-eyed, panicked Helen.

Rico emerged from the cell, shirt on, but unbuttoned. He picked up his tool belt and sauntered over to Helen. Tipping her chin with one finger, he kissed her full on the mouth.

Helen made little whimpering noises until Rico released her. "*Mañana,*" he murmured, eyes smoky. With a jaunty salute to Lizzie, he swaggered out of the Cells of Lost Souls.

Helen watched him go, knuckles pressed to her mouth.

Lizzie cleared her throat.

Helen's hands jerked down, and she flung a wild look at Lizzie. "I suppose you can't wait to tell Jared!"

Actually, she had no intention of embarrassing either Jared or herself by recounting this episode. "Tell him what? That I caught you smooching with Rico?" Lizzie shrugged. "No. It'd be too much like tattling."

Helen didn't appear as relieved as Lizzie expected her to be. Maybe Helen thought she was going to blackmail her or something equally stupid. "You aren't married yet, and Rico is attractive—in a primitive sort of way." Lizzie loved feeling superior for once. "Relax, Helen. I'm in a generous mood. You're off the hook."

She turned to go. What a wonderful story. She'd tell Carleen about it during their annual All Saints' Day unwinding blowout. Helen the Perfect, wasn't. Helen the Perfect owed her. Helen the Perfect was going to suffer over this. Helen the Perfect . . .

Helen the Perfect was crying. Great, gut-wrenching sobs wracked her body as she stumbled inside a cell and slumped against, appropriately enough, a torture rack.

All Lizzie's lovely feelings of superiority slipped away to be replaced by unwanted sympathy for her arch rival.

Keep walking, feet. She peered down. Her glow-in-the-dark skeletons did not move.

Rats. Heaving a great sigh, Lizzie spun around and trudged back to the sobbing Helen.

"E-lizabeth . . . I'm so miserable. What am I going to do?" Helen wailed.

Lizzie muttered something unhelpful.

Helen hiccuped and gazed at her hopefully.

Surely she didn't think *Lizzie* had the answers. "What do you *want* to do?"

"I want my life back the way it was!" Helen sniffed and dug in her pants pockets. Lizzie unzipped her fanny pack and offered her a tissue, but Helen had found a handkerchief. Monogrammed, of course.

"I already told you I wouldn't tell Jared, and I won't spring it on you in the future, either. It was just a kiss...." Lizzie trailed off as Helen began to cry again. "Okay, a couple of kisses. No big deal."

Sobbing, Helen shook her head.

"A few really terrific kisses?"

Helen chuckled through her tears, but when she covered her face with her hands, Lizzie knew there had been a lot more than kisses.

"Oh, Helen." This *was* a big deal. Lizzie joined her on the floor.

"I just couldn't help myself!"

"You've only known him, what? A week and a half? Two weeks?"

"Longer." Helen twisted the handkerchief. "I...I've been watching him. He... he and his crew were building my parents' cabana. I could see them from the music room. And it's been so hot." Helen paused and swallowed. "And he'd...they'd remove their shirts—" Helen broke off with a vague little gesture, which Lizzie understood perfectly. After all, she'd seen Rico herself. His muscles were a little overdeveloped, but Helen was obviously attracted to that sort of thing.

Lizzie wasn't, of course.

"At first I told myself I was only being kind," Helen continued.

"I'd call it more than that!"

Helen looked horrified. "I was referring to the iced tea and the lemonade and the sodas...and the beer at the end of the day. Well, I couldn't concentrate on my music anymore. I thought of Rico all the time. I couldn't even sleep. One day—"

"I don't think I want to hear this," Lizzie interrupted. "I mean, since Jared, my sex life hasn't exactly been..." Hasn't exactly existed, but why tell Helen? "I get the general idea." Lizzie propped her hand against the floor and started to rise.

Helen clutched her arm. "I have to talk to *somebody!*"

"Why me?"

"Because you're still in love with Jared."

Lizzie thumped back down, determined to admit nothing.

"Aren't you?"

She wasn't going to answer. *She* hadn't been dallying with a carpenter. Helen squeezed her arm harder. "I don't know what I feel for Jared," Lizzie mumbled, jerking her arm away.

"Oh, cut it out, Elizabeth. Let's be honest with each other."

Lizzie gazed into Helen's puffy gray eyes. They held weariness, but no insincerity.

"It's obvious you still love him," Helen said. "I might not have recognized love before, but I sure know all the signs now."

"I think you're confused by lust."

"Ha!" Helen swiped at her eyes. "I'm so far gone I don't even care! And you can't sit there and deny that you know what I'm feeling, because you feel the same way about Jared."

What Lizzie felt was close to tears. "Sometimes love isn't enough."

"Sometimes it's too much," Helen shot back. "Truce?"

With Helen? "What do we need a truce for? I already told you that I won't tell."

Helen smiled wryly. "A truce, because I don't see us as best buddies."

"Good point." Lizzie nodded slowly. "Okay, we have a truce, if you'll stop calling me Elizabeth."

"What am I supposed to call you?"

"I like Lizzie or Liz. Most people end up calling me Lizzie. Elizabeth is such a grand, important name. I don't think of myself as an Elizabeth. It's my stationery name."

Helen blinked. "But Jared calls you Elizabeth."

Lizzie blew the hair off her forehead. "Because he always wanted me to act like an Elizabeth. But he married a Lizzie." And that summed up four-and-a-half years of bitter arguments.

Now it was Helen's turn to nod.

"Every time he says Elizabeth—and *especially* when his mother says it—I hear a reprimand." Aghast at having admitted that to Helen, Lizzie stared at her clenched fists.

Helen was quiet a moment. "You know what I can't stand about his mother?"

Lizzie glanced up. She thought Helen and Jared's mother got along famously.

"She's always asking me to play the piano for her 'little gatherings,'" Helen continued. "And I always do. I pour everything into my performances."

"You play brilliantly."

One side of Helen's mouth tilted up. "Thanks. But all she ever does is give me a verbal pat on the head. 'That's nice, Helen, dear.'" It was a wicked imitation of Jared's mother's soft drawl. "You're the only one who's ever really reacted."

Lizzie cringed at the memories. "Don't rub it in."

"No. I appreciate it. Which is why I know you can understand how I feel."

That was lust logic—logic twisted by lust. "What I understand is that you're engaged to one man and sleeping with another."

Helen winced. "With Rico, I feel all the emotions I used to find in my music. Remember that day I brought you and Jared lunch?"

"Vividly."

"I meant every word about not wanting any emotional attachments. And this...this..."

"Affair?"

"Please." Helen groaned. "Whatever you call it has proved I was right. My music has fallen apart." Her hands clenched. "I used to visualize the notes soaring when I played. Now, they sit there like little lead pellets. I could see it coming. That's why I tried to get rid of Rico by sending him here."

"But you couldn't stay away."

"But I couldn't stay away," Helen repeated, her voice catching. "Oh, Lizzie, what can I do?"

She'd called her Lizzie. "Well, you can't carry on with Rico and still marry Jared."

"You said you wouldn't tell!"

"It's quite possible I'll regret that promise."

"I'll get over Rico." Helen's jaw set stubbornly. "I will."

Lizzie flung her arms in the air. "When?"

"I don't know."

She looked so wretched that Lizzie asked softly, "And why?"

"Because!"

"Because he's not *good* enough for you?" Like I wasn't good enough for Jared, she wanted to add, but didn't.

Helen was silent. Lizzie nudged her with a sneaker. "You expect me to disagree?" Helen asked.

Good ole Helen.

"Let's not discount our social, educational and cultural differences," she said. "Look what those differences did to you and Jared."

"Our only difference was that Jared wanted to be a snob and I didn't," Lizzie began acidly. "My family isn't listed in any social registers, but Jared and I have the same schooling."

"Sorry." Helen waved her handkerchief. "Truce, remember?"

Lizzie reined in her temper. "Your problem is between your head and you hormones. And until you decide which you're going to listen to, you have no business marrying anybody."

Helen began to sob again. Lizzie rolled her eyes and sighed.

"I can't give up Rico, but how can I tell Jared? *What* can I tell Jared?"

Lizzie had a few ideas, but prudently refrained from suggesting them. "Tell him you changed your mind."

Helen began violently shaking her head even before Lizzie finished speaking. "No. *You* tell him for me."

"No way."

"*Please*. He'll be so hurt."

Hurt? Jared hurt? His colossal pride, maybe. If he had any sense, he'd be relieved.

"You should have seen him after you left," Helen continued. "It was months before he recovered."

Lizzie sat very still. "I thought he wanted me to leave. I thought he hated me."

"No, the man was besotted. Lord knows why."

Lizzie smiled, even though she'd just been insulted. She couldn't help it.

"And you're as bad as he was," Helen declared in disgust. "*This* is what I have to look forward to."

Still grinning, Lizzie squinted down at her watch. "He'll be here in a few minutes. It'll be the perfect opportunity for you to talk with him."

"Or for *you* to talk with him."

"You first."

Helen drew a long, shuddering breath. "You're right." She got to her feet, Lizzie close behind. "You'll stick around and pick up the pieces, won't you?"

"Yours or Rico's?"

They stared at one another, then both began to laugh. Lizzie thought, for the briefest moment, that in another time and place—like another life and planet—she could actually like Helen Travis.

Twenty minutes later, Lizzie had paced and inspected every inch of the Cells of Lost Souls. Where was Jared? Hadn't Miss Fallen Angel told him where she was? Should she move on? She didn't want him to think she'd *expected* him to come to her.

On the other hand, he was now late for their appointment, and she would've been waiting impatiently, anyway. Should she pretend that she didn't know about Helen? Did Helen chicken out?

Or. . . or had Jared gone after Rico?

Lizzie dismissed that thought at once. Jared wasn't in love with Helen. Jared was in love with the *idea* of Helen.

Or had he been.

Lizzie paced nervously. This torture was worse than any dispensed by the instruments represented in the cells.

What was keeping him? How long could Helen draw this out?

Lizzie couldn't stand it any longer. Carefully stepping over the sound sensors, she retraced her steps to the backstage area where she wanted the shelves installed, noticing on the way that the black foam to pad the corners of the haunted house still needed to be put on. Lizzie made a note on her check sheet, her heart not really in it.

What if Jared arrived for their appointment and failed to mention his conversation with Helen? Lizzie couldn't say anything in case Helen left without speaking to him. In spite of their truce, Lizzie half expected Helen to slink off and leave the dirty work to her.

But what if Helen *did* talk to Jared, and Jared didn't mention it? That would mean he didn't want Lizzie back in his life.

Therefore, the only course of action Lizzie could take was business as usual, accompanied by an indifferent, ex-spouse kind of sophistication.

"Boo."

"Jared!" Lizzie started, entirely out of proportion to the quietly uttered word. "Did you see Helen? Did she talk to you?" So much for sophistication and reserve.

Jared stood at the other end of the hallway, saying nothing, obviously having no difficulty retaining *his* sophistication.

The dim lighting accented the shadows under his cheekbones and hid the expression in his dark eyes. He wasn't smiling.

Lizzie's heart began to pound at the exact instant Jared started striding toward her, his cast barely affecting his gait. She stood rooted to the spot, unable to speak, unable to move.

He walked right up to her, cupped her face with both hands, and kissed her—hard.

It was the kind of kiss that branded a woman as one man's. Possessive. Elemental. Not to be denied.

It was the kind of kiss that demanded an answer—and that answer had better be yes.

Lizzie felt the impact all the way to her toes, which curled inside the glow-in-the-dark skeleton sneakers.

Jared released her suddenly. She would have fallen, if he hadn't immediately hauled her close to him. "You're a witch," he whispered.

"I've been called worse."

"I can believe it," he said, as he lowered his mouth to hers once more.

Lizzie's notebook fluttered to the floor.

This time Jared's kiss was tender, seeking. Lizzie stood on her toes, wound her arms around his neck and kissed him back. If Jared was searching for love, he didn't have to look further.

Couldn't he see that they belonged together? Without her, he'd turn into a fossil. Without him, she had no anchor. Their very differences made them a stronger whole.

Slowly, Jared relaxed his grip, moving one hand underneath her hair and the other to the small of her back, where he insistently urged her closer.

Lizzie fit against him as if she'd never left. He was familiar and new at the same time.

Their three years apart had changed her, she knew, and now she learned that time had changed Jared as well.

Lizzie had developed enough self-confidence to stop constantly seeking Jared's approval on every aspect of her life.

And Jared had grown more accepting. Surely he must have, or he wouldn't kiss her this way, would he?

Would he?

He'd realized Helen was all wrong for him, hadn't he?

This was more than unrequited lust, wasn't it?

Lizzie's response became a little less wholehearted as she struggled with emerging doubts.

Jared sensed the difference immediately and broke off his kiss, dipping his head so he could gaze into her eyes. "I've wanted you from the moment you walked back into my life," he said with such conviction that Lizzie felt guilty for her thoughts. "You've felt the same way, haven't you?"

"Almost from the first," she admitted.

"But?"

"But there was Helen."

"Ah, Helen." Jared's mouth twisted.

"She *did* speak with you, didn't she? You're not still engaged, are you?"

"No."

"Well?" Lizzie waited.

Jared released her with obvious reluctance. "Let's sit down. I have a feeling we're due for a long talk of our own."

She closed the door to the backstage area, and they sat on the floor outside it, leaning against the matte black walls. An appropriate setting to discuss the ghosts of relationships past, Lizzie thought.

"I hope during our talk you plan to tell me how Helen finally corralled you into an engagement."

"I knew you were going to bring that up."

"She was all wrong for you. You're too much alike," Lizzie pointed out in case Helen's unsuitability hadn't occurred to him.

Jared slipped his arm around her. "Can't we just skip the talking and go back to kissing?"

Lizzie scooted a fraction of an inch away from him. "Not if it's me you want to be kissing."

"I had a feeling you'd say that, too." Jared regarded her wryly. "Helen made me an offer I couldn't refuse."

"Not her glorious self, I hope." Lizzie hugged her knees and stared at her tennis shoes. The glowing skeletons were fading.

"No." Jared gazed into the distance. "She offered entrée into the art world. Contacts. Potential commissions."

"You were going to marry Helen to further your architectural career? Oh, yuck!" A thought flickered through her mind. "Wait a minute—your parents love that artsy stuff. If you wanted contacts, you'd go through them."

"True," he acknowledged. "But Helen thought she had better contacts. I allowed her to think I believed that."

"Why?" Lizzie asked.

"So she could understand why I'd agree to enter into a marriage when I clearly wasn't in love with the bride-to-be."

"Why marry at all?"

"Because she wasn't in love with me, either."

"Oh. That makes perfect sense."

Jared paused briefly before he spoke. "Helen has some rather unusual views about love."

"Yeah, she told me all about them," Lizzie scoffed, then grinned. "Rico shot her theory all to pieces, huh?"

"Elizabeth."

"Lighten up, Jared."

"Hey, I've just been jilted."

"Does that mean she and Rico..." Lizzie trailed off suggestively.

"Are going to see each other openly, yes."

"Her mother's gonna have a cow."

"Elizabeth." Jared sighed her name.

"You had a lucky escape."

Jared looked at her sternly. "I do love Helen—as a friend," he added with a smile as Lizzie bristled. "We've known each other for a long time, and I think we could have had a comfortable life together."

"How *boring!* How could you settle for bland, predictable and boring?"

The smile faded from his face. "I never thought I'd fall in love again. I'd had my one grand passion."

"Me?"

Jared drew a finger across the freckles on her nose. "You."

Lizzie grinned, inordinately pleased at being called a "grand passion."

"You know what Helen said to me?" he asked.

"No, but I'm dying to."

"She said that she thought I regretted our engagement and subconsciously agreed to design this haunted house so I would have an excuse to call you."

"Our Helen's a clever girl." Lizzie slid him a sideways look. "Did you?"

He shrugged. "Maybe." Jared examined the black interior as if noticing it for the first time. "I would have married her, you know."

"Oh, I know. You *hate* admitting to a mistake."

During the silence that followed, Lizzie hoped Jared would try to prove her wrong by admitting that he'd made a mistake in letting her go. He didn't.

"So how does it feel to have your honey choose brawn over brains?"

"Don't be vulgar, Elizabeth."

Lizzie sucked in a breath that made her teeth freeze. *Calm down and don't overreact,* cautioned a small inner voice that was immediately drowned by a tidal wave of anger. "You've forgotten. I'm a vulgar person. In fact—" she stood and brushed off the seat of her pants "—I *enjoy* being vulgar. It's better than acting like my underpants have been starched!"

Jared laughed. Jared had never laughed at this point in their arguments before. He usually yelled something back at her. Lizzie had intended to exit stage right. "What's so funny?" she demanded instead.

"You. Your moods change faster than...than I don't know what. Seconds ago we were having an adult conversation." He stood, too, continuing to chuckle with an infuriating amusement.

Lizzie didn't miss the implication that she was acting like a child. Well, she didn't have to stick around and be laughed at.

"At least you haven't stomped off. That's an improvement."

Lizzie, caught in mid-stomp, pretended to examine the hinges on a door.

"The last time you stomped off, you never came back." A question sounded in his voice.

"I came back, all right. Helen was there."

He groaned. "Let's not talk about Helen."

"Why, when Helen was responsible for so many of our problems?"

"That's ridiculous." Jared's mouth set in a hard line. "And immature of you."

"Oh!" Lizzie sent a frustrated appeal skyward. "She *admitted* it."

Jared looked skeptical.

"She and your mother and her mother used every opportunity to make me feel inadequate and unsuited to be your wife!"

"My mother isn't responsible for your feelings of inadequacy."

Why wouldn't he understand? "I changed and changed and changed until I couldn't change anymore and still be me. That's when I realized that you didn't want me—you wanted a Helen clone!"

"Elizabeth—"

"*Don't call me Elizabeth!*" She covered her ears with her hands. "I'm not Elizabeth. I can't be Elizabeth!"

Lizzie closed her eyes to Jared's stunned face and blindly turned toward the exit.

He grabbed her arm.

"Let me go."

"Not this time."

He didn't say anything else until she opened her eyes. "This is the talk we should have had years ago, right?"

Lizzie nodded mutely, and Jared pulled her into his arms. "I'm listening now."

To her horror, Lizzie heard herself pour out years of pent-up frustration over petty slights. Incidents she hadn't even realized she'd remembered were trotted out and paraded in front of Jared. The meaningful looks passed between Helen and Jared's mother. Invitations that included Helen, but not Lizzie.

Jared still held her when she came to a shuddering halt.

"I wish I'd known," he said at last. "I *should* have known."

"I tried to tell you," Lizzie sniffed.

"Tell or yell?"

Lizzie ducked her head. It was only fair that she accept part of the blame for their breakup. A small part. She swallowed. Okay, maybe at least a medium part. "I can be emotional at times," she admitted grudgingly.

Jared tilted her chin until she gazed at him. "I enjoyed some of those times," he murmured before claiming her lips in a gentle, healing kiss that quickly warmed into something more.

"Ah, yes." Lizzie smiled a slow, wide smile. "We never had any arguments in this department, did we?"

"That's because we could shut out the rest of the world."

"I always thought of it as making our own world." Suddenly, Lizzie stood on tiptoe and flung her arms around Jared's neck.

She felt him stumble backward, but knew the wall was directly behind him.

"Hey!" He laughed and shifted his hold on her.

"We're alone now," Lizzie pointed out, allowing a sultry note to creep into her voice. She wiggled against him, pressed forward until he was trapped against the wall.

"You used to do this to me all the time," Jared said, tightening his grip on her. "Because you never expected me to take you up on your offer, did you?"

Lizzie squirmed, but Jared only held her tighter. "Did you?"

She laughed nervously. Come to think of it, he never *had* taken her up on any of her outrageous suggestions. He sounded as though that might change. Lizzie closed her eyes. It might be...

Awful. A vision of Rico and Helen flashed before her. What wretched timing. She'd think of them every time she was in this house. "Jared, we need to—"

"What's the matter... scared?"

Lizzie held her breath and released it slowly. "Lost the mood." She smiled weakly. "You called my bluff." Jared's arms loosened fractionally, but the challenge in his eyes never wavered. "We've got to make the inspection now. It's very late—in fact, I don't think I can make the last flight back to Houston."

"You're babbling."

Lizzie gently pushed out of his arms. "Yes, but it's truthful babble." She walked across the hallway, knees wobbling, and retrieved her checklist.

"Elizabeth..." Jared advanced with a purposeful gleam in his eye.

She squeaked and clutched the notebook to her chest. In seconds she was backed up against the opposite wall, one strong arm on either side of her. "Imagine, all these years you've been a tease at heart."

There was no answer to that. She ducked under his arm and ran.

He caught up with her in two steps, imprisoned her against the wall and kissed her thoroughly.

So thoroughly, the earth moved.

CHAPTER NINE

BUT THE EARTH SHOULDN'T have moved, no matter how powerful Jared's kisses were.

The wall quivered only a fraction of an inch, but Lizzie felt it and froze.

Jared raised his head immediately. "What's wrong?"

Lizzie stared at him without seeing, her thoughts on the wall. There had been too much bounce in it. She pushed away from Jared. The quiver became a wobble.

"I'm sorry. I thought we were kidding around." He stepped backward. "I...obviously misread your signals—"

"No." Lizzie gripped his arm. "You didn't misread anything." She traced her fingers over his lips in silent apology, then turned and kicked the wall.

It shuddered.

"What are you *doing?*"

"Testing." Lizzie rammed the wall with her shoulder. Then she took a running leap at it.

"Elizabeth!"

"The wall moved." She could hardly believe it herself.

"Of course it moved!"

"No." She shook her head emphatically. "Walls in my houses don't move unless they're supposed to."

"That's why we have inspections—to catch these problems. Make a note," Jared suggested, his voice calm and, she suspected, meant to be deliberately soothing. "We'll bring the carpenters back here and have them reinforce your wall."

Lizzie ignored him and the let's-humor-unstable-Elizabeth tone in his voice. It wasn't *her* instability he should be worried about.

She kicked the wall twice more.

"You're tearing the place apart!" Jared abandoned his fakely dulcet tones.

"Yes, I am, aren't I?" She examined the seams and joints. A gap large enough for her to slip her hand through yawned in the floor at the corner seam. The sick feeling in her stomach nearly overwhelmed her.

Jared grabbed her before she could ram the wall again.

"Let me go!" she demanded, twisting ineffectively.

"Why? So you can destroy everything?"

Lizzie jerked out of his arms, chest heaving. "Jared," she began, still breathing heavily. "Do you see that?" She pointed to the gap.

"Yes, you've knocked a hole in the wall!" He raked his fingers through his usually impeccable hair.

"I shouldn't have been able to."

"Congratulations, all those aerobic classes have paid off."

Lizzie didn't bother to respond. Leaving him staring after her, she walked down the hallway, bumping and ramming as she went.

Her shoulder hurt, so she used her hip. Soon that hurt, too. She sank to the ground and rested her head on her knees. This was a disaster. A full-fledged disaster.

"How bad is it?" Jared asked from above her.

At least he finally realized something was wrong. "This whole hallway will have to be rebuilt." Lizzie decided she'd give him the bad news in pieces, rather like the house itself would be once she finished knocking walls about.

"All right," he said, once again using his soothing voice. "It's an inconvenience, but not the catastrophe you're making it out to be."

Catastrophe. That was an appropriate word, too. Lizzie almost smiled, though she'd never felt less like it. Jared was making such an effort. Three years ago, he would've accused her of throwing a dramatic tantrum. The ironic thing was, if ever there was a time for wailing and rending garments, this was it.

"I've only inspected this one hall—"

"Are you saying you intend to wreak your havoc on the rest of my house?" Jared's carefully held patience slipped.

Wordlessly, Lizzie got to her feet and returned to the original gap she'd created. "Look."

"Yes, we've established that there's a slight gap."

"More like the Grand Canyon."

Jared inhaled and exhaled twice. "What else am I supposed to see?"

Lizzie squatted and fingered the sharp points of the nails that had torn loose. "These aren't the nails I specified."

"They're standard spec building nails."

"I don't use standard spec!"

"Of course not, that would be too easy and inexpensive."

"Jared, even you can see these nails are completely inadequate!" she snapped. "This is a wall opposite a fright zone. It has to be stronger than spec. It has to withstand hundreds of people bouncing against it."

"They're not going to ram it the way you did."

"Some of them do!" She stood—frustrated, tired, emotionally drained and scared. Scared of what she'd find when she tested the rest of the house. Scared of what it would mean to Jared. "I always specify nails with a hook at the end so they can't be pulled out."

Jared's mouth set in a tight line. "You must have forgotten to this time."

"That's extremely unlikely." Crossing her arms, Lizzie walked up and down the hall, checking joints and fittings.

She rounded the corner and stopped. "I don't believe this."

When Jared found her, she was kicking and pulling at a corner. "What now?"

"These two pieces are just *leaning* against each other!"

"We'll reinforce them," he said quietly, running his hand over the surface.

Lizzie turned her face away. She squeezed her eyes shut, swallowing rising panic. *I'm tired,* she reminded herself. *I overdramatize situations. I have to stay calm.*

She opened her eyes, then noticed something else. "The wood isn't the same. See—" she indicated "—this section is thicker."

Jared gestured to the thinner wall. "This was probably a piece from the original house."

Lizzie shot him a quick look. "I ordered all new wood."

Jared sighed and drew his hands up to his waist. "I accept the blame here. I recycled some walls in the interest of saving time."

Lizzie's eyes widened.

"Also," he pointed out, "this isn't a fright zone, so it won't have extra stress placed on it."

"But it shouldn't be leaning against the new section, either!"

"No, it shouldn't."

Lizzie fought for control. She heard the strain in Jared's voice and knew he was doing the same. He'd always remained in control. Unflappable Jared, able to diffuse her panics.

"Wasn't this area revised several times?" he asked.

How careful they were not to assign blame. My fault. Your fault. The carpenters' fault.

"Yes," Lizzie admitted, remembering the late nights. Remembering lines swimming before her bleary eyes. Remembering that Edward had offered to finish the drafting. "The wheelchairs couldn't pass through here easily."

"Can the thinner section remain, if it's reinforced adequately?"

Lizzie swallowed. Why had she never noticed that fire retardant paint made her nauseous? "Since it's not near a fright zone, I think it'll be okay. We'll make this a boo corner and have an attendant with a flashlight stationed here."

They smiled tight, relieved smiles at each other. Smiles that said, "See? This isn't so bad."

"Did you ... recycle any other areas?" Lizzie risked asking. *Please say no.* Jared's jaw steeled before he answered. "Quite possibly."

"Any idea where?"

"I'll have to consult my original plans and the various versions of yours."

Lizzie eyed him narrowly. Was he chiding her for her frequent changes? She could always counter with the fact that he hadn't told her everything she needed to know all at once. The mature action on her part would be to let it slide. Not nearly as satisfying, but more mature.

"I brought a set of plans with me." Lizzie unzipped her fanny pack and tossed him the keys to her rental car.

Jared snatched the keys out of the air. "Be back in a minute." A ghost of a smile played about his lips. "I suppose you'll continue bashing yourself against the walls."

"It would be easier if I had a crowbar."

Jared muttered under his breath. "I'll find some tools."

Lizzie couldn't wait for tools. As soon as Jared stalked out of sight, she continued deeper into the house. Just by knocking she could tell when the thinner wood was used.

She wanted to scream. She wanted to cry. She wanted to blame somebody. She wanted a magic wand and an extra week.

The thinner wood wasn't critical, she supposed. It would pass the city's engineering inspection. During a typical haunted house run, fifteen minutes out of every two hours was spent on repairs and reinforcements. Jared would have to schedule more frequent maintenance breaks. It meant fewer people could tour the house, but it would be safer that way.

Safety was everything. People could only relax and scare themselves if they believed they weren't in any real danger.

She tripped a sound sensor, the resulting growls irritating her more than they ever had. She ran through the rest of the house to the sound system electrical panel and disconnected it. Jared found her there, by the exit, moments later.

"Thanks." He hooked a thumb toward the control panel.

Lizzie managed to laugh. "We'll pay later. It'll probably never connect properly again."

Jared squatted on the floor, cardboard tubes bouncing from his arms. "I found the carpenters' blueprints, too."

Lizzie found the emergency flashlight and held it aloft.

In the murky pool of light, they studied the plans. Fifteen minutes later, they still couldn't agree on which set was current.

"*I* have the latest updates," Lizzie said. She'd said it before, too. At least twice.

"Yes, except . . ." Jared followed a hallway with his finger. "Here. I changed that."

"When?"

He shrugged. "Last week sometime."

"Without telling me?"

"I meant to."

Lizzie stared at him in disbelief. "You changed my plans without telling me? You wouldn't have done that to any other architect, would you?"

"Probably not," he agreed, quietly.

"You didn't trust me."

"The changes shouldn't have made that much difference."

"But they did, didn't they?" Lizzie couldn't believe it. She wanted to throw something. Something rotten and squishy.

Instead she looked at Rico's plans. "At least *he* knew about the changes," she said with asperity. She pointed. "That explains the nails. You didn't specify the hooked nails on this change order."

"My mistake."

Jared admitting he'd made a mistake? Lizzie was relieved that it hadn't been *her* mistake. "Rico should have caught it, even if he hasn't built a haunted house before."

"Apparently Rico had other things on his mind," Jared said dryly.

Hadn't they all, Lizzie thought and cleared her throat. "But the right nails weren't used in this area, either." She traced another hall.

Jared compared his own plans with hers, then Rico's. "Look."

The nails were specified on his plans. But not on Lizzie's updates.

Her eyes widened—enough to see Edward's initials in the corner.

"Edward." Lizzie shook her head. "He knows better." How could Edward have forgotten to specify the correct nails? Lizzie answered her own question. Because they'd been in a hurry. Too much of a hurry. In fact, Edward might have assumed that Jared already had the nails.

No, Lizzie wouldn't blame Edward, but he was definitely going to hear about it. She was to blame for even taking on this job. She'd known they would feel the pinch of too much to do in too little time.

Jared's words interrupted Lizzie's self-recriminations. "The nails are specified on Rico's version of the plans."

"What version does he have?" They both searched for the date.

"Hard to say." Jared flipped through pages with different dates.

It appears that Rico had been building from a number of different sets of plans.

"Anyway, the nails should have been ordered before you began construction," Lizzie said.

"We ran out."

"How could you run out? I purposely ordered—"

"I thought you ordered too many."

Lizzie's mouth dropped open. "You aren't about to tell me you reduced the order, are you?"

Jared nodded. "And—" he massaged his temples "—I remember sending one of the volunteers to buy more nails."

"I see." There didn't seem to be anything else she could add.

For hours, Jared and Lizzie compared plans, bashed walls and searched for flaws until dawn pinked the Dallas sky.

"The house cannot open as it is," Lizzie said in a weary voice. She was tired of arguing. She was tired, period.

Walking out the entrance into the fresh air of a new day, she inhaled deeply.

Fresh air did nothing for her headache. Or her grimy skin. Or her fuzzy teeth.

"This house *will* open." Jared, his beard-roughened chin jutting, followed her outside.

"I don't see how." They'd discussed this over and over for the last hour.

Jared refused to admit defeat. "You're responsible for this. What do you intend to do about it?"

Lizzie gasped. "*I* am not totally at fault here!"

"You and your devoted assistant."

"You leave Edward out of this! I take full responsibility for his mistakes. But not *your* mistakes!"

"I don't need anyone taking responsibility for my mistakes."

Lizzie smiled triumphantly. "So you finally admit that you made mistakes! That's with an '*s.*' More than one."

Jared opened his mouth, then checked his response. "Listen to us. We're bickering like a couple of kids when we need to be thinking of a way out of this mess."

"Okay, I say block off the back half and use the front half. Cut a new exit."

"No."

"Well, that's my recommendation."

"Half the house would be nothing!" Jared exploded in anger. Lizzie had been expecting him to yell for so long, she was relieved he'd lost his temper at last. "We couldn't charge enough admission to cover the expenses. The patrons might as well have given their money directly to the clinic!"

Lizzie exhaled, shoulders slumping. "That's the only thing I can come up with right now. That or rebuild the entire back portion of the house. You have two days, three if you count Halloween itself."

"We can't rebuild this house in three days. You'll have to think of another way." His challenge rang in the early morning stillness.

"No, Jared. *You'll* have to think of another way. I've had it with this project. I warned you we didn't have time for mistakes. Now you refuse to take the only way out." She gestured impotently. "I can't help you anymore. I've got final inspections pending all over the state."

"Have your assistant..." Jared snapped his fingers as he struggled for the name.

"Edward," Lizzie supplied harshly.

"Edward can make your inspections."

"Edward's already making inspections."

"Have him make some more, then! There can't be all *that* many!"

"Well, here's a news flash for you. There are." Lizzie straightened her shoulders. "But I'm not surprised you don't think I have any other responsibilities. That's the way I've acted, isn't it? I've been at your beck and call since you asked for my help. I've made so many trips to Dallas, that the flight attendants don't even ask me what I want to drink—they automatically bring me club soda!"

She spun around and began walking to her car. "You have no idea how much time I spent on this project at the expense of my other commissions."

"I certainly hope you weren't as sloppy with their plans!" Jared shouted after her.

She stopped walking and glared at him. "What a nasty thing to say!"

"What did you expect? We've hit a snag—"

"A snag? You call this a snag?"

"—and you're running away. But isn't that how you've always dealt with problems?"

Lizzie crossed her arms in front of her. "Dragging our past differences into this isn't going to fix your house."

"No. But I think our 'past differences,'" he echoed her words, "are responsible for our present situation."

"Go on," Lizzie prompted.

"I know you," he said with quiet emphasis. "In spite of your eccentricities, you're a good architect. You've built a reputation as an expert in this field."

"Thank you," Lizzie replied, knowing he hadn't intended to compliment her.

"Which is why I must assume that the capricious changes, incomplete plans and hastily drawn modifications were deliberately calculated to publicly humiliate me."

Multisyllabic words. A sure sign that Jared was rip-roaring mad.

Tough. He could just stay rip-roaring mad. Lizzie stepped forward and planted her chin inches from his neck. "Cow puckie."

He blinked. She was so close she could almost feel the breeze from his lashes.

"Very mature of you, Elizabeth."

"It's a favorite expression of eccentric people." Lizzie invaded his space a moment longer, then regally strode across the parking lot to her car. If she sped—just a wee bit—she had a chance of making the first Southwest airline flight of the day. Unfortunately, she was now flying standby and early morning flights were crowded with business travelers.

She was a business traveler, too, wasn't she? She simply wasn't dressed like one. Brushing at the gray smudges on her rumpled slacks only produced smeary streaks.

"Just a minute, Elizabeth." Jared stalked toward her.

"Haven't got a minute."

"One question, then you can leave."

Lizzie indicated that she was willing to listen.

"Did you plan for this to fail from the very beginning?"

Traffic rumbles from the awakening city receded. In the gray-pink light, Jared's eyes blazed with anger. His forbidding expression might have been carved from granite.

He believed she had sabotaged the haunted house.

In that moment, any possibility of a future with Jared died. Not even when they'd divorced had Lizzie thought their relationship was finished. But his question implied that he truly believed her capable of plotting a revenge that would hurt not only him, but a clinic for the injured and disabled as well. He believed that she was a person who would sacrifice her integrity and reputation to hurt him.

And he believed it in spite of all the tender words he'd spoken. In spite of wanting her. And now she knew he didn't want her. He wanted the physical relationship they'd shared during their marriage.

But that hadn't been enough then, and it wasn't going to be enough now. For three years, Lizzie had tried to earn Jared's respect. She'd obviously failed.

Her heart flash-froze. She'd thaw it out later, when she was alone. For the moment, she would focus on leaving with a measure of dignity.

"What do you mean?" she asked, though she knew exactly what he meant. Lizzie just wondered if he'd actually say the words.

He would. "I mean," he enunciated distinctly, "did you deliberately sabotage this haunted house project to humiliate me?"

"Humiliate you?" Lizzie repeated dully.

"Yes. You were jealous because I was engaged to Helen. You've always been jealous of Helen."

He waited for her to say something. He probably thought she'd yell and leave.

And perhaps she would have—before—when she could still feel.

"Jared, did you deliberately sabotage this haunted house project to publicly humiliate me?"

"*What?*"

Lizzie tried to think like Jared as she formed her response. "I thought it very out-of-character for you to choose—voluntarily, I understand—to design a haunted house. And I asked myself why? Did he finally recognize the importance of my work? No," she answered her own question.

Lizzie paced and continued talking, as if to herself. "He wanted to use volunteer labor. He altered plans without telling me. He neglected to provide pertinent information affecting the design. He ignored my purchase orders." She glanced up to see if Jared was paying attention. He was.

"On his own, he reduced the amount of materials ordered. It never occurred to him to trust my judgment. That perhaps I might—oh, radical thought—know more about this subject than he did." She glared at Jared, who now looked more uncomfortable than angry.

"And he seems to have forgotten that it's *my* reputation that will suffer when this house doesn't open!" Lizzie ended her pacing directly in front of Jared.

Jared closed his eyes for a long moment. "I apologize and can only plead exhaustion." He draped a hand on the back of her neck and briefly massaged the knotted muscles.

Lizzie said nothing and tried not to enjoy the warmth of Jared's hand.

"What is it?" he asked when she remained silent.

"I'm waiting for you to plead stupidity."

Jared dropped his hand. "Come on, Elizabeth. You made a few mistakes yourself."

"Yes, I did. My biggest one was taking on this project in the first place. There wasn't enough time. I should never have accepted it."

"Then why did you?"

Shrugging, Lizzie decided to tell him. There was no reason to hide it anymore. "To impress you. So you could see that I have a real business. A legitimate business. That I made something of myself when you didn't think I could."

They stared at one another. Jared raised his hand, then let it fall to his side. "I had no idea that my opinions mattered to you one way or the other."

If she didn't leave soon, Jared would figure out *why* his opinions mattered to her.

The sun shone above the buildings in the Dallas skyline, gilding the haunted house and chasing away ghosts.

It was time for Lizzie to chase away ghosts of her own. "You influenced me as I built my business," she admitted. "And it's that business that I have to protect now." She stuck out her hand, hoping for a businesslike conclusion to the shambles of their project. To the shambles of their relationship.

Jared grabbed her hand. "You aren't leaving!"

"I have other responsibilities."

"What about your responsibilities here?" He spun her around so she faced the forlorn building.

Ice cubes. Her emotions were ice cubes. "You can't open this Halloween, but you'll still have the structure once you make the modifications. Plan to open next Halloween for the entire month of October and you'll raise enough money to make up for this year." She forced a smile. "Check with me in the spring. By then, I'll be free to devote one-hundred percent of my time and energy to the Hanes Memorial Haunted House." By spring she might even be over him.

"You're serious." Jared stepped away from her. "You're going to leave."

Lizzie nodded. "Remember the Haunted Hotel?"

"Sure. Your big project. The one that's supposed to bring you fame and fortune. Make your name a household word."

She decided to ignore his sarcasm. "I have an appointment there at ten-thirty." She raised her wrist and thrust her watch in front of his face. "I'm going to be late."

"Fine!" Jared shoved her arm aside. "Go. I don't need you." He backed away. "If half the house has to be rebuilt, then I'm going to rebuild it. And the entire Hanes Memorial Haunted House *will* open on Halloween—no thanks to you."

After three steps, he stopped and asked, "Tell me, though, if I were a regular client and not your ex-husband, would you still leave right now?"

Her heart began to thaw as hot tears spurted into her eyes. Blindly, Lizzie made it to her car and unlocked the door. "If I weren't your ex-wife, would you insist that I throw away my entire business on a doomed project?"

"Exaggerating just a bit, aren't you?"

She hated the patronizing tone in his voice. "If anything, I haven't emphasized my position enough. I have contractual obligations to fulfill. If I break them, I'll never be hired to design another haunted house. Anywhere. *That's* what I have at stake." She choked on a sob. "As it is, I'm jeopardizing the most important commission I've ever had! And all for you, Jared!" Lizzie yanked open the car door and climbed inside. "Would you put your architectural firm on the line for that?" She pointed out the window to the house.

"For a haunted house? Of course not," he snapped, glancing at it with derision.

"You're asking me to."

"Because it's your business to haunt houses!"

Lizzie smiled crookedly. Jared would never consider designing haunted houses as important as his own commissions.

He confirmed it seconds later. Approaching her car, he gripped the open window edge, his arms fully extended. He bowed his head for a brief moment, then looked her straight in the eyes. "We've both said some harsh words we haven't meant."

Lizzie briefly reviewed their various exchanges. "I meant everything I said. Just what didn't you mean?"

"You'd like to see this house open, wouldn't you?"

Lizzie cautiously nodded.

"Your other houses have passed their local building codes, right?"

"Yes, but—"

"Then they can open if you don't inspect them personally."

"Maybe, maybe not. I have no intention of finding out by abandoning them."

"Don't worry." Jared opened the car door. "I won't let you starve if you lose clients over this."

"I'd lose everything over this."

"No problem. You'd come work for me."

For him? Not with him? "But you don't design haunted houses."

"Thank God!"

"I like designing haunted houses," she maintained stubbornly.

"Elizabeth." Jared stopped talking and smiled at her. She didn't smile back. "You've made your point. Very well. You were able to support yourself. Truthfully, I didn't think you could, even though that was our main source of income when we dissolved our partnership. I didn't then, and don't now, think this fad will last. I'm offering you a graceful way out."

She didn't want a way out, graceful or otherwise. "And if this . . . fad does last?"

He shrugged. "You've outgrown it. Time to move on." He gestured for her to get out of the car.

She stayed put. "What if I don't want to move on?"

Annoyance flashed across his face. "My firm will not design haunted houses and frankly, your personal commitments will prevent you from doing them."

In a few sentences, he'd reduced her hard-won architectural firm and reputation to an annoying personal entanglement.

Lizzie gestured across the parking lot. "What do you call that?"

"Temporary insanity, caused by the pain medication I was given. Now stop being temperamental and get out of the car!"

"No!" Lizzie took advantage of his stunned surprise and jerked the door closed. "My business is as important to me as yours is to you. My designs are as much a part of who I am as yours are of you."

Jared stepped back from the car without commenting. Lizzie wasn't even sure he'd heard her.

"I know that in spite of my recommendation, you're going to try to rebuild that house in time for Halloween."

"And I will." The way he vowed it almost had Lizzie believing it was possible, almost convinced her to stay.

Almost.

"Good luck," she said.

"Good-bye," he corrected, then added. "If you change your mind, call me."

CHAPTER TEN

LIZZIE WATCHED JARED saunter into the house. He'd deliberately echoed her parting words of three years before, she knew he had.

They'd come full circle, and this was where she was going to get off. She slammed the steering wheel with her fist, which did absolutely nothing for her peace of mind—and hurt, besides.

"Jared is a jerk." That had a nice, alliterative ring to it. She said it again. "Jared is a jerk."

And Lizzie was in love with him, so what was she? Yes, she still loved him—for precisely those reasons that made him a jerk.

The most infuriating thing was the guilt she felt because she wasn't going to hop out of the car and run after him. She had responsibilities. Commitments. A business.

And he expected her to throw it all away!

His breathtaking arrogance made her too angry to cry.

She drove away from his haunted house knowing that he'd push himself to exhaustion so it could open. And why? Because Jared Rutledge was a man of his word. He'd told the clinic they'd have a first-rate haunted house, and he'd see to it that they would, even though he considered such work beneath his talents, an opinion that went a long way toward maintaining his jerk status.

All she'd wanted was his respect for her chosen career, and she'd jeopardized that very career in order to get his respect. As if that wasn't bad enough, at some point during this whole fiasco, she'd managed to delude herself about their having another chance together.

Now, she didn't have his respect or his love. And if she didn't hurry back to Houston, she wouldn't have her business, either.

It was all his fault, she told herself, sobbing into her next-to-the-last tissue as she waited at a toll booth. Why couldn't he have left her alone? Why on earth had he thought of designing a haunted house?

And how much longer would it take her to get over him? To let go? To accept the fact that Jared felt one way and she felt another?

She'd tried to change his opinions about haunted houses. And he'd tried to change her mind about her career goals. It was history repeating itself. In fact, during their marriage, Jared had tried to change a great deal more than her mind.

Why couldn't he love her for who she was? *She* wouldn't insist that he design haunted houses to the exclusion of anything else—like those stark, stuffy buildings of his.

But, a thought niggled at her, wasn't she always trying to get him to loosen up? Wasn't she trying to change him as much as he changed her?

During the hour-long flight, on which she'd managed to get a ticket by bursting into tears at the gate, she remembered all the little things she'd done when they'd been married. Like the time he'd asked her to pick up some of the white shirts he liked.

White shirts were boring, she'd thought, instead buying Indonesian batik.

Jared favored well-crafted antique furniture. Lizzie countered with Zulu war masks. Jared designed buildings with strong, clean lines. Lizzie told him they could be improved with a gargoyle or two.

She slumped in her seat, equal parts misery, guilt and regret. For a few, brief glorious moments, she'd thought they were going to try for a life together again. Now she knew that even if Jared was still willing, and she highly doubted it, she couldn't return to the life of an Elizabeth.

As soon as the plane landed, Lizzie called a worried Carleen.

"Where are you?"

Closing her eyes, Lizzie leaned against the wall next to the phone. She couldn't help noticing how solid the wall was. "I'm at the airport. Call the Haunted Hotel people and warn them I'll be late. I've got to shower and change."

"You can't."

"Carleen, I've been up all night. Jared's house was a disaster. *Is* a disaster. I look like garbage." She felt like garbage, too.

"'Hello Houston' sent their camera crew to the ghost town *today*. Right now. They called to see if you could come early."

Lizzie gritted her teeth. "'Hello Houston' was supposed to film on Halloween."

For the first time since she'd hired her, Lizzie heard Carleen lose her temper. "You would have known about the change *if* you'd bothered to check in!"

Carleen was right, of course. Lizzie rubbed her eyes and thought longingly of a hot bath. "Can you stall them?"

"What do you think I've been doing since eight o'clock?"

Precious seconds ticked by. "Tell them I'll leave directly from the airport."

Lizzie hung up the phone and headed for the restroom where she splashed water on her face and arms, then stared in the mirror. Her reflection was frightening. TV. She was about to appear on the popular Houston morning program resembling a debauched corpse. Moaning, she sought the bright lights of the airport gift shop.

Makeup, toothbrush, toothpaste, chocolate. All life's basics. Clothes. Hers were in wretched condition. She'd buy a giant T-shirt and hope it covered everything that might appear on camera. Flipping through the racks, she discovered her choices were "Don't Mess with Texas," "Somebody in Texas Loves Me," the Houston Oilers, Astros, and an armadillo frolicking in bluebonnets. Within minutes, Lizzie and the armadillo were on their way to the Haunted Hotel.

"HELLO, HOUSTON! This is Maria Alvarez on location at the Haunted Hotel in the southwest's newest tourist attraction, a ghost town, outside of Richmond. Here with me is Elizabeth Wilcox, who designed the scary structure."

Maria, of the white smile and plastic hair, turned to a caffeine-and-chocolate-fueled Lizzie. "Elizabeth, tell us how you became involved in designing haunted houses." She thrust a bulbed microphone in front of Lizzie.

With false brightness, Lizzie babbled her much-told story about collaborating with Jared in college. She mentioned nothing about their most recent collaboration and was pleased that her voice didn't break.

After answering a few more routine questions, Lizzie took Maria and the home viewers on a tour of the Haunted Hotel.

As she stressed safety features, Lizzie didn't see the walls of the Haunted Hotel, she saw the splintered separations in Jared's house. When she fingered the black foam used to protect people from painful bumps, she recalled that Jared still had it to install. Would he remember?

During the entire tour, Lizzie thought of Jared doggedly persevering. Here was the triumph of her career, and she was thinking of Jared. Would she ever be free of him? More to the point, did she want to be free of him?

"What about children? Are there any age restrictions on who can tour your houses?" Maria asked.

"Yes," Lizzie answered, grateful Maria had asked before Lizzie had to introduce the subject. "We recommend that children aged eleven and under do not go through the Haunted Hotel."

"Why is that?"

"They become too scared. They don't enjoy it. And yet, we still have parents who insist on dragging small children through. A child of five or six can't separate reality from make-believe."

Maria donned a face of professional concern. "But the ghost town is for families. What can the younger children do?"

Lizzie smiled. Maria had done her homework. "That's why we have the Kiddie Corral." Lizzie led the way to a room on the ground floor of the hotel. "Attendants will staff this room at all times. Children can play here while their parents and older siblings tour the hotel."

Pointing to a table, she explained, "We'll have face painting, a maze, a cartoon room, funny mirrors and treats."

The camera panned the room, with Maria making her closing remarks and urging people to attend the grand opening on Halloween.

Once they'd finished, Lizzie shook Maria's hand and limply collapsed on a tot-size chair in front of the funhouse mirrors.

How lovely she looked. Huge head, long skinny neck, gigantic hips on toothpick legs. Just the way she felt. She craned her neck in order to see past her blackened knees, the same knees she hoped hadn't appeared on camera.

When Mr. Gelfin, the ghost town manager, found her, Lizzie was lifting up her foot in its glow-in-the-dark skeleton tennis shoe and admiring the leering skeletons in the mirror.

"Maria Alvarez was very complimentary. 'Hello Houston' will feature us on their Halloween morning show." Mr. Gelfin seemed both pleased and vaguely disapproving.

"What about the grand opening? I thought they were covering that?" She'd dress every inch the professional. Even Jared wouldn't be able to find fault.

Mr. Gelfin shook his head. "Schedule conflict. We'll probably draw some of the local news teams, though, unless Halloween is a big news day."

So much for professionalism. Lizzie gestured to her frolicking armadillo. "I'm sorry, I didn't realize they were coming. I drove here directly from the airport, and I've been awake all night." She chuckled. "I'll have to watch the show to find out what I said."

Mr. Gelfin gurgled in alarm.

"Kidding," Lizzie assured him. She stood and motioned to the mirrors. "These mirrors need to be lowered. They're for children, yet I couldn't see my feet when I was sitting there."

"Drat those mirrors," Mr. Gelfin said with feeling.

"Why?"

He ran his hand over the bald spot on the top of his head. "First, Fun House Supply sent us all the same ones. Then they got the order right, but they sent two of each mirror. Now I've got to send those back."

Lizzie nodded absently, preoccupied with her own problems. How fast could she shower and inspect her two Houston houses? She needed to coordinate with Edward, too. A nap wouldn't hurt, either. In fact—

"I said, how far down should we position these mirrors?" Mr. Gelfin, usually mild mannered, sounded testy.

"Sorry." Lizzie sat in the tiny chair and pulled out a tape measure. "If I were a little kid, I'd be about this tall..." She gazed at her reflection in one mirror, then dragged the chair to the next. "I need wheels on this thing," she commented to Mr. Gelfin. He didn't smile. What a grump. "Move the mirrors all the way to the floor and—"

Lizzie stared at herself. At the chair. Wheels. *Wheels!* She jumped up. "That's it!"

"What?" asked a startled Mr. Gelfin.

"A Kiddie Corral!" Lizzie flung her arms around Mr. Gelfin in an exuberant hug.

"Ms. Wilcox!"

"Don't you see?"

"Not—"

"Jared needs a Kiddie Corral! The back half of his house can be a Kiddie Corral! Or a . . . a Kiddie Crypt! That's it, a Kiddie Crypt!" Lizzie clasped her hands and spun around.

"Who is Jared?"

"It doesn't matter." She wobbled unsteadily and vowed to never spin on an empty stomach again. "You said you still had the extra set of mirrors?"

"Yes."

"I'll buy them from you."

He blinked in bewilderment. "Well, I . . ."

"Come on, Mr. Gelfin, you were returning them anyway."

Still flustered, Mr. Gelfin adjusted his glasses. "I suppose it would be all right. . . ."

"Oh, thank you!" An elated Lizzie kissed the startled Mr. Gelfin on the cheek.

"CARLEEN!" LIZZIE bounded into her office. "You've got to buy some stuff for me."

Carleen peered at her over the tops of her rhinestone cat eyeglasses. "My, don't you look nice. Does this mean you'll be returning that special 'Hello Houston' suit you bought?"

"No, I'll save it for the 'Goodbye, Carleen' party."

Carleen grinned. "Am I going somewhere?"

"Yes, shopping." Lizzie thrust an airline ticket envelope at her. "I made a list."

Carleen squinted at the scribbling.

"It's a little messy. I jotted it down at traffic lights."

"'Face painting kit, ten plastic pumpkins, two gross of balloons, ribbons, a tank of helium'?" Carleen glanced at Lizzie, then continued reading, "'Glow-in-the-dark worms, ten strings of Halloween lights, skull rings, yucky plastic wiggling things'?"

Lizzie nodded. "For prizes. You know, spiders, bugs, that sort of thing. Like for a kids' Halloween party."

Carleen pointed. "Baseball bats?"

"No. Bat bats." Lizzie flapped her arms.

"Oh. Would these be live bats?"

"Carleen! Plastic ones—for the bat toss."

Carleen's lips formed a silent Oh. "One never knows with you, Lizzie."

"Ha. Ha. Where's Edward?"

"If he's smart, he's hiding." Carleen ran a finger down the scheduling calendar. "He's supposed to be in Austin, then Lubbock."

"I thought we'd done the inspection in Lubbock."

"The Lubbock civil engineer had some questions."

"Hasn't he ever heard of the telephone?" Lizzie grumbled. That's all she needed, more problems.

"You weren't here, and we had to decide—"

"Never mind," she interrupted. "When Edward checks in, have him come home by way of Tulsa, Oklahoma."

Carleen made a note. "And where are you going to be?"

Lizzie climbed up the stairs to her apartment. "Dallas."

"Oh, no."

"Don't worry. I'll catch the houses here and reschedule Edward."

"I don't know," Carleen cautioned. "You've already given him a full load."

"Tell him too much sleep is hazardous to his health." Lizzie was still put out over the careless mistakes Edward had made on Jared's drawings. "Just the other day, I heard about an exhausted architect who strangled one of her sleeping assistants after she'd been awake all night coping with one of his mistakes."

"Uh, oh. How bad?"

Lizzie stared into the distance, seeing the Hanes Memorial Haunted House. Seeing an equally exhausted, but determined Jared. "Jared's house might not open."

Carleen gasped.

"But I have an idea," Lizzie continued. "Scrounge up whatever you can from that list. I'll finish looking in on the Houston houses and fly back to Dallas."

"What about the Haunted Hotel?"

"Since 'Hello Houston' has filmed their segment, it won't matter if I miss the hotel opening."

"Miss the hotel opening! But Lizzie, you wanted—"

"It's okay." Lizzie closed her eyes and swayed. That shower better revive her. "Check the list and see if I've forgotten anything."

Carleen raised an eyebrow. "A partridge in a pear tree?"

Lizzie laughed. "Wrong holiday."

"Tell that to the stores. I swear, it'll be easier to find a partridge than Halloween supplies this close to Halloween." Carleen opened the file cabinet and removed her purse. "Shall I stick around to make sure you don't fall asleep?"

"No," Lizzie said with determination. "You can bet Jared won't be sleeping. And if he can stay awake, *I* can stay awake."

"WAKE UP, JARED!"

A groan—human this time—echoed through the Hanes Memorial Haunted House.

"Sneaking a nap in a coffin? How macabre of you." Lizzie shined a flashlight directly on his face.

He winced. "On the contrary. I thought it highly appropriate. Save time later."

"For what?"

"Funeral arrangements."

"Jared!" Lizzie roughly shook his shoulder.

"I feel horrible." Two dark bleary eyes gazed at her reproachfully. "This isn't heaven, is it?"

"Where are the carpenters?"

He squinted at his watch. "I sent everybody home. Elizabeth, what are you doing here? It's eleven-thirty at night."

"Didn't you get my message?"

"Skip the middle and start from the exit? Yeah, I got it."

"Well?"

"Close the lid on your way out."

"Jared Rutledge, get out of that coffin!"

"It suits my mood. Why are you here, anyway? Postmortem?"

"I have come to solve all your problems," Lizzie announced majestically.

"You're hallucinating. Sleep deprivation will do that to you."

Lizzie leaned against the coffin. "You've given up, haven't you?"

"You did, too, so don't sound so sanctimonious."

"I quit, because you refused to compromise. Now, you've given up."

Jared raised himself, lifting his arms theatrically. "So I've seen the light! Which I wish you'd point in another direction."

Lizzie moved the flashlight beam. "This isn't like you, Jared."

"I suppose," he said, slowly climbing out of the coffin, "the absurdity of it all finally hit me. Here I was, frantically working on a *haunted house* for you."

"For *me?*" Lizzie gaped at him. "It was *your* idea in the first place."

"But then it became your design. And I could see how great it was going to be. All our advertising proclaims this as a Wilcox house. If we only open half a house, people will be disappointed." He swiped at the seat of his pants. "It's better that we don't open at all."

Lizzie's heart, tired, bruised and battered though it was, thumped. "You were doing this for me?"

Jared stretched and smiled lopsidedly. "Well, there was a certain amount of pride involved on my part, too."

"Pride in a haunted house?"

Jared's grin widened. "Yeah. Beat you at your own game. Fix the house when you said it couldn't be done."

She poked him with her elbow. "Wanted to show me up, huh?"

Nodding, he ran a hand over his beard. He looked dangerous with a beard. She liked dangerous.

"I thought you had inspections. What happened?"

"I inspected," she informed him. "It's amazing what you can accomplish when you don't waste time sleeping."

Before Jared could make any reply, the low rumbles of an approaching vehicle caught Lizzie's attention. A horn beeped twice.

"It's here." Lizzie ran to the doorway. "C'mon, Jared."

"What's here? Who's that?"

An airfreight delivery truck rolled to the front of the clinic. "Over this way!" Lizzie called.

The driver backed up and squeaked to a stop.

"What have you done, Elizabeth?"

Elizabeth. Still. She shrugged it off. "Help the man unload while I sign for this."

Lizzie scrawled her signature, ironically the same Elizabeth she detested.

Jared questioned her no further, simply carrying boxes into the main entrance of the haunted house.

"Let's check the packing list," Lizzie suggested after the truck had driven off.

Jared shot her a this-had-better-be-good look and flipped open his penknife. After slicing the brown tape on one of the boxes, he peered inside. "Am I looking at a box of bugs?"

"Describe them."

Wordlessly, Jared held up one.

"Beetles. Four gross." Lizzie checked it off the list. She peered into the box, forehead wrinkling. "Does that look like four gross of beetles to you?"

"You want to count?" Without waiting for her answer, Jared sliced open another box. "I can't make out..." He gasped.

Lizzie smothered a snicker.

"*What* is this?"

She shined her flashlight toward the jellied mass, then turned the light off. The mass glowed an eerie green. "Worms," she explained. "Glow-in-the-dark worms. Neat, huh?"

"Words fail me." Jared indicated the rest of the shipment. "Explain."

And Lizzie did.

"The middle will be blocked off?" he questioned.

"Yes, and we'll cut a new exit."

"You don't think people will feel cheated?" Jared continued opening boxes as she talked, which Lizzie took as a good sign.

"We're offering something for everyone—how could they feel cheated?"

He straightened and studied her for a long moment. "Will this be a house you'd be proud to lend your name to?"

"Absolutely," Lizzie assured him.

The expression on Jared's face changed subtly. Hope. He was allowing himself to hope.

"It's different from your other houses," he remarked, cautiously.

Lizzie wanted to jump up and down, demand he call the carpenters out in the middle of the night and blast full steam ahead. In fact, she'd often accused Jared of being a stick-in-the-mud, of dampening her enthusiasm. For the first time, she realized that he was thinking through all the possibilities and pointing out those he thought might not have occurred to her.

And, she admitted, in the past, she'd often acted impulsively. Imprudently. But this time, she *had* thought things through.

"Yes, it will be different. I considered that. But this house has been built for people with physical limitations, and that's already something different. The public will be expecting changes. I have a children's area in the Haunted Hotel. I'd like to experiment on a smaller scale. This is the perfect place."

She stood quietly, letting him think.

Jared chewed on his lower lip. "It's tempting." He shoved his hands into the back pockets of his pants.

"And you've bought all this stuff," he said, nudging a box with his bandaged foot.

"Yeah." Lizzie scooped up a handful of skull and spider rings, letting them dribble back into their box. "Wouldn't want to let it go to waste."

They gazed at each other. "Déjà vu," Jared said, softly.

"All over again." Lizzie grinned.

"Halloween is the day after tomorrow."

Lizzie pointed to her watch. It was after midnight. "Tomorrow."

Exhaling forcefully, Jared let his head fall back. "I must be out of my mind!"

"Wouldn't be the first time."

Jared looked at her sternly.

"Well?" Lizzie cocked an eyebrow.

"Elizabeth," he said, beginning to laugh, "call the carpenters!"

CHAPTER ELEVEN

"*QUADRUPLE* OVERTIME? You promised the carpenters *quadruple* overtime? I've never heard of quadruple overtime!" Jared, seated on a child-size plastic seat, stared up at Lizzie as if she were crazy.

"How else did you think I could get them here in the middle of the night?"

"It's morning now," Jared grumbled.

Lizzie bent and kissed his nose. "You're so cute when you're angry."

"Wait until you see him after I finish painting this little pumpkin on his cheek," Helen said, dipping her paintbrush into orange paint. "Hold still, Jared. I need practice for tomorrow night."

"You tell him, Helen."

Jared narrowed his eyes.

"Quit squinting, the pumpkin is wrinkling."

"It's practically in my eye!"

"I can't help it!" Helen protested. "Your beard's in the way."

Lizzie walked behind Helen and peered over her shoulder. "You've got a real flair for face painting."

Helen leaned back and admired her design. "I do, don't I?" She glanced up at Lizzie. "Oh," she said, tilting Lizzie's chin. "Hold on." Helen dabbed her brush on a cloth and changed paint colors. "I'm better at whiskers now."

Lizzie felt coolness as the black cat on her cheek grew whiskers. She caught Jared's incredulous expression.

"Aren't you two supposed to hate each other or something?"

Lizzie looked at Helen.

Helen looked at Lizzie.

"No," they said, shrugging almost in unison.

"People change," Lizzie said, as Helen returned to Jared's pumpkin, though privately she admitted that the strain of trying to "out nice" Helen was getting to be too much.

"Oh, no. I'm not involving myself in that old argument and forgetting about the quadruple overtime."

Lizzie snapped her fingers. "Curses, foiled again."

"What were you thinking of?" Jared doggedly pursued what he perceived to be an extravagance on her part. "How can we justify the expense?"

Lizzie sat in a seat opposite the face-painting table. "We pay only *if* Rico and his crew finish reinforcing the main children's area by noon. They just get double for the rest of the job."

"How frugal of you."

"Rico can do it, too," Helen said with confidence. "There. One pumpkin. I've got the hang of this, I think."

Jared examined his pumpkin in the mirror. "Lopsided," he pronounced.

"*You* try to paint on a moving canvas!"

"It's beautiful, Helen," Lizzie interrupted, amused to find herself peacemaker. "Will you be able to stay this afternoon?"

Helen gathered her brushes, rags and paint. "Sure."

Lizzie stood, using the table as support. She'd better stop sitting down. It was becoming too hard to stand up again. "I'm going to call my secretary and visit the two other houses I have in this area. If nothing goes wrong—" she crossed her fingers "—I'll be able to come back here and help you decorate."

Jared stepped in front of her, blocking the exit. "When was the last time you had any sleep?" he asked, studying her with suspicion.

"Oh..." Lizzie fluffed her curls and widened her grainy eyes, hoping she looked energetic and alert. "I slept on the plane."

"At the most, two hours in two days." Jared made a disgusted sound. "*I'll* drive you to your other houses. You'd probably fall asleep on the freeway."

She'd probably fall asleep at a stoplight before she ever made it to the freeway. "I'll be fine," she insisted.

Jared grabbed her arm just above her elbow and steered her toward his car.

"I can drive myself," she protested, even though she didn't really want to. "You're needed here."

"Not as much as *you* need me right now."

She loved it when he took charge. Sometimes, she'd get herself into such tangles, but Jared would always manage to untangle her. However, being an independent woman, she wasn't supposed to enjoy it. "And how much sleep have you had?"

"More than you."

"Only if you count your nap in the coffin."

He ignored her. "Where to?"

Lizzie sighed in surrender. "Arlington, then Plano."

Jared opened the door to his incredibly comfortable-looking car and pointed. "Inside."

Since Jared was having one of his macho attacks, she might as well humor him. Besides, the car had such a soft plush interior. Headrests... A warm shoulder...

"HAVE I TOLD YOU how wonderful you are?"

She was still dreaming. And it was the most delicious dream. . . .

Jared kissed her eyelids, then her cheek and the side of her neck. Lizzie opened her eyes and found two brown ones, above a slightly lopsided pumpkin, watching her.

"Jared?"

"How do you feel?"

Lizzie groaned. "Like I've been hit by a truck."

"Good, then you're awake."

The dream? "Were you kissing me just now?"

"Do you mind?"

"I don't think so."

The pumpkin swam out of focus as Jared bent to kiss her again. Lizzie closed her eyes, her arms entwining themselves around his neck. She lost herself in a fuzzy emotional cocoon. There was only Jared.

She could forgive anything when she was wrapped in Jared's arms. She could forget anything and everything. She could . . .

Jared broke the kiss. Lizzie whimpered in protest and held on to keep him from moving away. "I'm glad you came back," he whispered, gently smoothing her curls off her forehead. "I was so angry after you left. First at you, because you'd dared to leave me, then when I'd calmed down, I was disgusted with myself because I'd been . . ." He gestured mutely.

Lizzie shifted, so his face was in focus. "Are we talking about yesterday or three years ago?" she asked sleepily.

"Could be either, couldn't it?" Jared sighed and rested his forehead against hers. "As soon as this is all over . . . whether or not the house opens—"

"It will," Lizzie insisted.

"Whether or not it opens," Jared repeated. "And after we've both had some sleep, we'll talk."

"About us?"

He nodded. "I don't want to lose you again."

Lizzie murmured her agreement and settled against him.

Jared chuckled and disentangled himself from her arms. "Time to go."

"Go where?" Lizzie blinked at him in confusion, then suddenly remembered everything. She jerked up, nearly crashing into his head, and looked around. They were in Jared's car in the Hanes Memorial Rehabilitation Clinic's parking lot. "What time is it?" Panic nearly overwhelmed her as she tried to focus on her watch. "Jared, why did you let me sleep? I *told* you I—"

"Shh." He placed a finger against her lips. "We've gone and now we're back."

They'd driven all the way to her other houses? Lizzie rubbed her temple. "I don't... Jared, you're not lying to me, are you?"

He grinned. "You fell asleep before I started the car. I drove to Arlington and when I couldn't wake you, I inspected on your behalf. Everything was great, everybody was thrilled. I wished them good luck and drove to Plano. There, I actually got you out of the car, but it was obvious that you weren't your usual perky self, so I repeated the routine, then drove back here."

"Thanks. I think." Lizzie shook her head, trying to clear it. She was beginning to feel better. Hungry even.

"Rico and his crew earned their bonus."

"Great. What's left to do?"

They climbed out of Jared's car into the early evening. He massaged his injured foot and grimaced. "We have to rewire the electrical system, finish installing the padded corners, decorate the children's area, add more lighting, hang black-out drapes to keep the light from shining into the front part of the house—"

"Hey, good thinking. Whose idea was that?"

"Mine."

When had he found time? "How long did I sleep in your car, anyway?"

"We've been back here about an hour."

And he'd let her sleep. "Thanks, again. How about the painting?"

Jared nodded and began walking toward the house. "Yes, there's still a few places that need to be touched up. Helen's painting now. Rico and his crew have left to sleep while the electrician wires the house."

"How about the city's electrical inspection?"

"Tomorrow morning." Jared winced. "I owe everybody."

He limped toward the entrance, and Lizzie felt a pang. He was exhausted. "Jared, you sleep now."

He shook his head. "Can't." He gestured toward the car pulling into the parking lot. "That'll be the electrician."

But the slight blond man who emerged from the car was no electrician.

"Edward!" Lizzie exclaimed when she saw her bleary-eyed assistant. "What are you doing here?"

"Carleen tells me I'm single-handedly responsible for all the ills that have befallen you."

"You had help," Jared said expansively.

Edward smiled, his relief obvious. "Nevertheless, I'm here to make amends." He bowed, swaying a little.

"You look awful," Lizzie told him.

Edward's gaze flicked from her to Jared. "Then I'll fit right in."

They entered the house, discovering that Helen had nearly finished the painting.

"Edward, you remember Helen," Lizzie began. "Jared's..." she trailed off, searching for the right word.

"Friend," Helen supplied easily.

Friend. Lizzie tried on the word and decided that amazingly enough, it fit.

With Edward's arrival, Jared was able to sleep until midnight, when the carpenters returned. Lizzie convinced Helen to go home and sleep so that she could assume her face-painting duties when the house opened for business.

At dawn, Lizzie drove to the townhouse she'd once shared with Jared to shower and change.

As she slipped the key into the lock, Lizzie wondered what she'd find.

A sense of the familiar washed over her as she gazed around her. The differences were subtle and few. She might never have left.

Or lived there in the first place.

Jared had collected a few new antiques. A sideboard filled the space once occupied by her drafting table. The Zulu war mask that had once hung in his dining room and now resided in hers, had been replaced by a mirror.

Her ethnic throw rugs had been replaced by one gorgeous oriental. It looked great, she admitted wryly.

Jared had reupholstered one of the chairs. As Lizzie recalled, the original fabric had been a busy geometric pattern that had appealed to her, but didn't seem to go

with anything. Now the slate blue leather enhanced the
masculine richness of the room.

A few pillows, some rugs, knickknacks, wall hang-
ings...she'd thought she'd been expressing her indi-
viduality and all she'd done was clutter up the place.

Lizzie wandered into the master bedroom. Subdued,
tasteful. New curtains. New bedspread. She opened the
closet to a long row of pristine white shirts. Lizzie
shoved them to one side. At the very end of the rod, she
found the batik shirts, still as crisp as the day she'd
bought them, obviously unworn.

She'd had absolutely no effect on his life at all. The
whole house shouted, "This is Jared's home! No tres-
passing!"

Panic set in when she tried to imagine living here
again and couldn't. She knew Jared was going to suggest a reconciliation, and she'd been agreeable until
she'd stepped through the front door.

Now she knew it was impossible. How could she
move back to Dallas? And Lizzie knew without a
doubt, that she would have to be the one who moved.

What about her business? Edward would find another job, but what about Carleen, her one-in-a-million
secretary? Carleen's family and children lived in Houston. She wouldn't consider leaving them.

And was Lizzie ready to give up designing haunted
houses? Jared had made it absolutely clear that he
didn't want to be associated with haunted houses. The
troubles they'd had with the clinic's house would only
reinforce his decision.

Lizzie walked into the bathroom and turned on the
shower. They were at an impasse. They faced the same
problems that had driven them apart three years ago.

Nothing had changed. Lizzie stepped into the shower, her tears mingling with the spray.

"HURRY!" HELEN URGED. "People are lining up outside!"

"A lot of people?" Lizzie asked, peering through one of the brand-new exits.

"Yes, considering that it's not dark yet."

"All right!" Lizzie stopped Edward from carrying his armload of debris out the front. "Preserve the illusion, Edward. Haul that stuff out the back."

"Would that be the illusion of organization?" Jared asked, touching one of the walls. "Uh, oh. The paint isn't quite dry."

Lizzie rubbed her hand over the wall and studied her palm. "It doesn't seem to be coming off."

"Jared," a skeleton called. "We're all in place."

"Okay." Jared took a deep breath. "Elizabeth? Ready for the run-through?"

Lizzie crossed her fingers, then she and Jared walked outside the house to the entrance.

The line of people had grown in the few minutes since she'd last looked. Twilight glinted off half-a-dozen wheelchairs. "We're almost ready," she called as she and Jared met Danny, the skeleton, at the entrance.

"Break a leg," Lizzie said.

"She doesn't mean that literally," Jared advised.

Darkness enclosed them as the door shut. Immediately, a white figure leapt out at them, startling them deeper into the house.

"Exactly right," Lizzie murmured in approval.

They groped around corners and through rooms. "Even though I know every inch of this house, I feel disoriented," Jared said, just before he stumbled and fell against Lizzie.

She heard metallic clanking.

"It's a toolbox!"

"Grab it and we'll take it with us," Lizzie instructed. "It's not in the plans."

They made it through the rest of the house without another incident. Monsters growled when they were supposed to. Actors ran the special effects with perfect timing and the shortened house seemed to be just the right size.

When they emerged into the purpling dusk, they signaled Danny to let in the first group of people.

In the back half of the house, Helen painted pumpkins, spiders, cats and ghosts on chubby cheeks. Rico manned the bat toss and filled balloons with helium.

Lizzie and Jared wandered toward the lone tree on the clinic grounds. Earlier, they'd set up chairs so they could watch as people ran screaming from the exit, scaring those who were waiting to enter.

Lizzie would have liked more separation between the children's area and the exit, but all things considered, she was grateful they'd managed to open. As a steady stream of cars and vans poured into the clinic's parking lot, Lizzie began to relax.

"Looks like we've done it." Jared dropped the toolbox and collapsed into a folding chair.

Lizzie's legs gave way a moment later.

"Is this how you always spend Halloween?" Jared asked.

"Nope. I'm usually checking out the competition."

"Competition? I thought you had a monopoly on Halloween."

"Oh, no." She slid a glance sideways. Dusk had turned to night, making it difficult to read his expression. "There are others just as frivolous as I am."

"You aren't going to let me forget I said that, are you?" He draped an arm around her shoulders.

Lizzie took a deep breath. It was time for their talk. Much as she enjoyed this companionable harmony, she knew it couldn't last. "I think it's the root of our problems."

"Would it help if I told you I realize how important all this is to you?"

Lizzie's foolish heart beat faster. "Yes."

"And that I'd never ask you to give it up?"

Tears threatened. "You wouldn't?"

"No." He kissed her lightly. "If you want to design haunted houses, then design them."

The tears overflowed. He finally understood her.

"And during your off-season, you can design more conventional houses."

He sounded so reasonable. Right up until the last. "I don't have much of an off-season," she sniffed, hoping he'd take the hint that she never intended to design anything remotely conventional.

He didn't. "Oh, Elizabeth," he whispered, gathering her into his arms. "Will you marry me...again?"

Elizabeth. Nothing had changed. Lizzie's heart twisted, and she shoved him away. She couldn't put herself through the pain again. "I can't, Jared," she said, sobbing. "I just can't."

She had a glimpse of his astonished face before she lurched to her feet and ran, pushing her way past the line of waiting people until she reached her car.

Jared caught up with her as she fumbled for her keys.

"Jared, your foot!"

"Yes, it aches like fury!" He grabbed her keys.

"Give me those!"

"Not until you tell me why you're running away."

Lizzie scrubbed at her cheeks. "Because it won't work. It didn't work then, and it won't work now. We're too different and too stubborn. All we'd do is hurt each other."

He looked stunned.

Lizzie took advantage and pried her keys from his unresisting fingers. "Good-bye, Jared." She wanted to wish him happiness and a good life but didn't trust herself to speak.

"I love you, Lizzie. I always will."

Lizzie froze. "What did you say?" Her heart pounded in her ears. Maybe she'd just imagined it.

"I said I love you." A corner of his mouth tilted. "Didn't you know that?"

"What did you call me?"

Jared's forehead wrinkled, then he shrugged. "Lizzie. It slipped out."

"You called me Lizzie," she said, first in wonderment, then with glee. "You called me Lizzie!"

"Almost everyone does."

"But *you* never have."

"Elizabeth is a beautiful name. I suppose Lizzie suits you more, though."

"Just the way you're a Jared and not a Jerry."

As they stared at one another, Lizzie could see the exact instant understanding came to Jared. Of course it helped that he also smacked the hood of her car with his open palm. "That's where we've gone wrong, isn't it?"

Lizzie, tears clogging her throat again, could only nod.

"Well, let's get this all out in the open." Jared ticked off points on his fingers. "Number one. I love you." He waited until Lizzie realized she was supposed to say something.

"I love you, too."

"Do you?"

"I said I did."

"I like order, neatness and tailored clothes. Gargoyles do not belong on my buildings. I'm willing to try new things...but not every single day. And I reserve the right not to like some of the new things I try." He breathed deeply. "Now, do you still love me and not your idea of me?"

"Yes," she said, meekly.

"All right. Number two. I have no wish to merge our architectural firms. I can either live with you or work with you, but not both. Agreed?"

"Yes," Lizzie said again. "But where will we live?"

"I'm coming to that." He paced the length of the car, then returned to stand in front of her. "You seem to have a lot of business in Dallas, and I've had several commissions in Houston. So, when I'm in Houston I'll stay with you. When you're in Dallas, you stay with me."

"Jared, a commuter marriage!" Lizzie smiled in delight. "How unconventional." She wrinkled her nose. "I like it."

"I thought you would," Jared said with a smile of his own.

"What made you think of it?"

"I couldn't bear the thought of that Zulu war mask leering at me as I ate breakfast every morning for the rest of my life."

Laughing, Lizzie flung herself into his arms. "I'll hang it over the fireplace."

"Even better." His head bent to hers, but just before she closed her eyes, Lizzie was distracted by the molten glow of the rising moon.

"Jared, look. It's a perfect Halloween moon."

He kissed her anyway, then looked. "What a setting. A full moon, a haunted house, assorted spooks and goblins... Lizzie, now will you marry me?"

"What about your mother? My parents will be thrilled, but—"

"My mother and Helen's mother will have a glorious time commiserating with each other over the folly of their children. They'll be impossible until the grandchildren arrive."

"Grandchildren?" Lizzie asked tremulously.

"*If* you'll marry me," Jared prompted with impatience.

"Yes!" she said, knowing that this time their marriage would last.

As they clung together, Lizzie thought she'd burst with happiness. All too quickly, he set her away from him and tilted his watch until he could read its face in the moonlight. "Come on." He grabbed her keys and unlocked the car door.

"Where?"

"We can be in Houston by nine o'clock. Just enough time to catch the grand opening of your Haunted Hotel."

Dazed, Lizzie slid into the car. "Are you sure? I could go by myself."

"Oh, no." Jared started the car. "If we're going to have a commuter marriage, we might as well start practicing now."

"But how can we do this with children?" she asked in a small voice.

Jared tossed her a grin as he backed the car out of the parking lot. "We'll deal with the little goblins when they arrive."

At that, Lizzie Wilcox screamed.

For joy.

Take 4 bestselling love stories FREE

Plus get a FREE surprise gift!

HARLEQUIN ROMANCE®

A Halloween treat that's better than candy and almost as good as a kiss!

Two delightful frightful Romances from two of our most popular authors:

HAUNTED SPOUSE by Heather Allison
(Harlequin Romance 3284)
"Frizzy Lizzie" the Scream Queen confronts her handsome ex-husband—over a haunted house!

TO CATCH A GHOST by Day Leclaire
(Harlequin Romance 3285)
Zach Kingston wants to debunk Rachel Avery's family ghost. Rachel objects—and so does the ghost!

Available in October—just in time for Halloween!—wherever Harlequin books are sold.

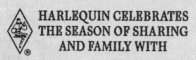

1993 Keepsake

Stories

Capture the spirit and romance of Christmas with KEEPSAKE CHRISTMAS STORIES, a collection of three stories by favorite historical authors. The perfect Christmas gift!

Don't miss these heartwarming stories, available in November wherever Harlequin books are sold:

ONCE UPON A CHRISTMAS by Curtiss Ann Matlock
A FAIRYTALE SEASON by Marianne Willman
TIDINGS OF JOY by Victoria Pade

ADD A TOUCH OF ROMANCE TO YOUR HOLIDAY SEASON WITH KEEPSAKE CHRISTMAS STORIES!

HX93